MW00772716

Then Ananias answered, Lord, I have heard by many of this man, how much evil he hath done to thy saints at Jerusalem.
Acts 9:13 KJV

KC Hart

Our Head Strong Love

Red Creek Redemption Book 1

Also By
KC Hart

A Christmas Blaze

Fresh Starts and Small Town Hearts

Business Smarts and Reckless Hearts

Car Smarts and Bashful Hearts

People Smarts and Wounded Hearts

Kid Smarts and Wistful Hearts

Family Smarts and Runaway Hearts

Elsie: Prairie Roses Collection

Moonlight, Murder and Small Town Secrets

Music, Murder and Small Town Romance

Memories. Murder and Small Town Money

Merry Murder and Small Town Santas

Medicine Murder and Small Town Scandal

Marriage, Murder & Small Town Schemes

Mistaken Murder & Small Town Status

Mistletoe, Murder & Small Town Scoundrels

Join KC's newsletter and receive a free ebook of Music Smarts and Humble Hearts

If you enjoy my books, please consider leaving a review where you purchased them. Reviews help an author in so many ways.

Blessings,

KC Hart

Chapter One

L ucy Robinson lifted her enormous dark shades and stared at the swanky hotel on the side of the interstate. That had to be the place Gordon was talking about, the hotel where she would be working, the Blue Hotel. Her truck eased to the right lane as she passed by and took the exit, heading toward Red Creek, Alabama. She pulled her glasses back into place and ran her fingers through the top of her head, fluffing her curls. No one would recognize her. After all, it had been twenty-three years. She glanced down at the front of her blouse as her truck eased to a stop at the end of the exit ramp. She had definitely changed... in more ways than one.

Lucy turned onto the blacktop road and glanced again at the expensive looking hotel. It towered head and shoulders above everything else around it, including the parking lot full of vehicles. She would come back in a bit and check in. First, she wanted to drive through the town, see what had changed, what was the same. The hotel disappeared in her rear-view mirror, and rows of pine trees mingled with the occasional home filled the scenery as she made her way toward Red Creek.

She slowed the truck, creeping along the two-lane road to the edge of town. The garment factory appeared off to the right, signaling she was entering the Red Creek city limits. She and other women from the town had spent many an hour in that warehouse, leaning over sewing machines, making a little above minimum wage. It was one of the few places girls with only a high school education could get a job.

Her eyes widened. "Well, I'll be." The once dismal brick building, with dirty windows and only box fans to circulate the air, had gone through an amazing transformation.

Gordon had filled Lucy in on her daughter's plans to buy the old garment factory and turn it into a restaurant, but this —this wasn't some little hole in the wall mom and pop diner. No, apparently her only daughter had a touch of Lucy's tendency to dream big, to want more. The old red brick building now had enormous clay urns overflowing with greenery and bright flowers on either side of the black metal door. A snazzy black and white striped canopy covered the entrance. A string of fancy white twinkle lights ran up the side of the building and along the edges of the canopy, giving the place an upbeat, welcoming vibe. This place would appear at home on any street in a big city. Red Creek had definitely moved up in the world.

The best part of the building, the part that made Lucy's heart swell, even though it had no right to, was the bold cream-colored sign above the entrance below the second-story windows. *Ollie's Family Restaurant,* written in a beautiful loopy font, was painted in shiny black letters. Would her only daughter hate her when she found out she was back in Red Creek? Would she welcome her home? Or worse yet, would she be indifferent, treating her like any other stranger? Like she was simply one of the new influx of tourists going through the little town on their way to the Alabama coast?

A car sped around Lucy and she jumped, startled out of her wool-gathering. She pushed on the gas pedal and headed into the town. She crept down the street, taking in the old and the new. Gordon's office, the Blue building, stood in the spot that had been the feed store when she left twenty-three years ago. She would circle back soon and tell Gordon she had arrived, but first there was one place she needed to see.

Lucy stopped at the corner, shoving her shades closer to her face as a gray-haired couple walked down the sidewalk, peering at her through her windshield. Everyone would know soon enough that Lucy Robinson, the prodigal wife and mother, was back in Red Creek. For today; however, at least for a while, she wanted to stay invisible.

His place, their old place, looked exactly the same, well, almost. The enormous metal sign hanging across the front, *Robinson Junk & Salvage,* had a few more layers of burnt orange and deep red rust eating through the metal making it hard to read. It didn't matter, though. All you had to do was look at the place to know it was a junk store. The same junk store she had walked away from years ago.

"Six months, Orville. That's all. If I can't make it by the end of six months, I'll be back, and we'll never talk about me being a singer again." Lucy cleared her throat, refusing to let the memory affect her, drag her backwards. *I'm a new creation in you, Lord. Please let my family see the new me—and forgive the old me.*

She slowed the truck to a stop on the quiet street and looked at the parking lot full of holes holding water from a recent summer storm. The place was obviously closed, but that didn't mean he had shut down the business. It wasn't quite ten, and Orville had always been a little lax with hours of operation. How he scraped out a living selling other people's

3

castoffs was pretty amazing. *Does he look the same? Has he changed as much as I have?*

A horn tooted behind her, and she moved forward, driving her truck away from the building that housed so much of the past she had tried to put behind her. She continued through the rest of town, noting the changes and the things that would never change. She scanned the sidewalks and the storefront windows, searching for familiar faces. The boys, all men now, of course. Did they take after him? Oscar, their oldest, had to. He was born looking like a carbon copy of his father. The other four had been more of a mixture, except for Ori. He had favored her with his fair hair and grey eyes. Did he still? The twins, so young when she drove away, would she even recognize her youngest son and only daughter?

She looped through the rest of the town and pulled her truck into a park in front of the Blue building. She flipped down the visor and stared at her reflection in the little mirror. "Definitely not the same girl that left." Pulling a tinted lip gloss from her purse, she ran it across her lips with practiced ease. "Time to step out of the past and into the now. Lord, give me courage." Her phone buzzed, and she pulled it from her purse and looked at the screen. "Go away, Cal. What we had is long gone." She hit ignore and dropped the phone back in her bag.

Lucy hopped out of the truck and hurried into the office building, her gauzy baby blue skirt flowing around her thin frame. She pushed open the glass door and strolled up to the reception desk. "I'm here to see Gordon Blue."

The woman looked up from her computer and smiled with practiced politeness acquired from years of working with the public. "Do you have an appointment?"

"No." Lucy pulled her shades from her face. "Tell Gordon his fiancé is here."

Orville pulled open the door to the sheriff's station and blinked, waiting for his eyes to adjust to the dim fluorescent lights inside. Oscar, his oldest son, stood behind him, waiting for his father to enter.

"I can handle this, Dad, if you want me to." Oscar followed Orville inside, and his eyes roamed around the cinderblock walls. "You can go open up the store."

"No. I'm his father." Orville pulled in a deep breath and patted his shirt pocket for a piece of peppermint. "I'll take care of it." He pulled the candy out and started unwrapping the paper as the sheriff, a round man with a pink bald spot and horn-rimmed glasses, stepped into the little lobby from his adjoining office. "JT." Orville nodded at the man he had known ever since grade school. "I'm here to see Ori."

"I hate I had to bring him in, Orville." The sheriff pulled a key ring from the desk drawer between the men. "But Les said your boy threw the first punch. Cory went through the big picture window, so I'm sure Les will get in touch with you about paying for all the damages."

"Not me." Orville popped the candy into his mouth. "This is the third time I've bailed that boy out. If he owes the man money, he can pay for it himself. Maybe then he'll learn to stay out of the bars." Orville followed the sheriff into the back and stared at his son, bent forward on the cot, his head in his hands. The sheriff lifted the key to the lock and Orville placed his hand on the man's shoulder. "Give me a few minutes, JT."

The sheriff glanced through the bars at Orion Robinson as he rose from the cot, then turned to Orville. He slipped the

5

keys down, not unlocking the door. "Holler when you're done. I'll be out front with Oscar."

"You know what I did yesterday evening when we closed the store?" Orville stepped closer to the cell bars.

"No, sir."

"I hoed the garden. I worked out there until I couldn't see what I was doing. Then I came in, ate supper, read my Bible, and went to bed." Orville stared through the bars, watching his son run his hand through his sandy blond hair. The boy was too good looking for his own good and had a tongue as slick as a fish-belly. "You know what I like about working in the garden, son? Why I plant the tomatoes and the corn and the peas?"

"I guess to keep everybody fed."

"That's part of it, but what I enjoy about making a garden is that it's predictable. I put the seeds in the ground and take care of them and they do what is expected. They grow and they produce. I don't have to worry about the plants when I'm not around. They're dependable. They will produce to their full potential."

"Dad, you know what kind of mouth Cory Walters has. I gave him plenty of warnings, but he wouldn't shut up." Ori's fists clenched and unclenched. "If you'd been there, you would've done the same thing. The guy was harassing Ella Jo Sellers, Floyd's daughter. What was I supposed to do? Let him keep doing it?"

"Son." Orville raised his eyebrows. "The point is, I wasn't there. I was home where I was supposed to be, where you should have been. You're not a kid anymore, Ori. I'm not going to bail you out. You got into this mess; you'll have to get out of it."

"Dad." Ori's eyes stretched wide. "I'll pay you back and work something out with Les. It's not that big of a deal."

"The first time wasn't that big of a deal. The second time I warned you." Orville shrugged his shoulders. "I'm done, son. If you don't get your life right with the Lord, you're headed down a rocky path."

Orville turned and walked from the room, ignoring the sound of his son's fist slamming against the bar. Some people could only learn the hard way. His son was one of those people.

Oscar waited with JT in the front lobby. "Come on, Oscar. I need to stop by the post office and drop something in the mail. I'm already late opening the store." Orville looked at JT. "Call me if you need me."

Oscar followed Orville to his ancient truck and climbed into the passenger's side. "If you need to borrow some money to pay his bail..."

"It's not about the money. I've got the money." Orville slammed his squeaky truck door and started the engine. "It's about your brother owning his problems. I'm praying that if he has to clean up his own mess, he will think twice about throwing his fists."

"Aren't you being a little rough on him, Dad? You know Cory Walters is a jerk."

"There are a lot of jerks in this world. Ori has to learn to deal with them inside the law." He slowed his truck as he passed by the Blue building. "Your brother needs the Lord."

Oscar leaned forward and looked at where his father was staring out the side window. "Who's that woman kissing on Gordon Blue? I don't think I've seen her around here before."

"I'd know her anywhere." Orville nodded as the woman finished kissing Gordon Blue on the cheek and looked in their direction. "That woman is your mother."

Chapter Two

Lucy felt his eyes watching her as she pulled away from Gordon. His truck, the same truck he had when she left, crept past... and there he was. His striking blue eyes met hers, his piercing stare in his tanned face held her gaze as he eased further away. He nodded, letting her know he recognized her, like there was ever any doubt that he wouldn't. They'd always been that way, like two magnets knowing the other was there, pulled toward the other before they even knew what was going on.

"Looks like the cat's out of the bag."

"Huh?" Lucy turned as the truck disappeared around the corner. "Oh, yes." She smiled at Gordon, his arm still draped around her shoulders. "I guess it is."

"Do you want me to go with you to see him?" Gordon pulled his arm away and walked Lucy to her truck. He nodded at another truck passing by. "We can go this afternoon before he leaves his store."

"No." Lucy waited while Gordon opened her truck door. "I need to do this by myself." She glanced down at the ring on her finger, then up at Gordon. He was such a kind man and a dear friend. She had to get everything settled, for his sake. "Once I explain to him how we started seeing each other and about our plans, he'll sign the papers. He can be reasonable."

"I know." Gordon held her arm as Lucy stepped up into her pickup. He watched her settle in behind the wheel. "I just worry. There's a reason he's never signed your divorce papers."

"It's because I did him wrong, and he's an ornery old bear. Once I apologize and explain that I'm not the person I was, he'll do the right thing." She rolled her lips in and bit down. "He has to."

"I hope you're right." Gordon shut the truck door and smiled as Lucy rolled down the window. "Orville Robinson has a stubborn streak a mile long."

"Believe me, I know." Lucy turned her cheek to Gordon as he leaned through the window and kissed her goodbye. "He'll either listen to reason, or I'll—well, he has to listen to reason. I don't love him, he doesn't love me, the kids are grown. There's no reason in the world for him to refuse to sign those divorce papers."

Orville watched Oscar turn and stare out the back glass of his pickup until the Blue building and Lucy were out of sight. "Do you want me to drop you by your office?"

"No, sir." Oscar twisted back around and faced his father. "I'll get out at the post office and walk back."

"I'm not going to the post office."

"I thought you said..."

"I changed my mind." Orville looked straight ahead through the glass, his jaw firm. "I've got to get to the store.

Some people have to work for a living. Do you want me to drop you off or not?"

"No, sir. I'll walk from the store." Oscar's brow furrowed, and he glanced over at his father. "Why do you think she came back after all these years?"

"I guess she came back to kiss on Gordon Blue. That's what she was doing." An old country song started playing on the radio, and the lyrics floated from the speaker. *No matter what I give, no matter what I do, I don't think it'll ever be enough to pay the cost of loving you.* Orville reached over and snapped off the radio.

"Do you think she'll come by to see us?" They pulled into the junk store parking lot and Oscar waited. He watched his father's face as he put the gear stick in park. "I mean, I was what? Eight years old when she left. I remember her, and Owen does, but the rest of them, they probably don't even remember her ever being our mother." His brow pulled low. "I don't like this. She can't just come back home like she never left."

"Well." Orville turned and looked at his son, a younger version of himself in so many ways. "She's a grown woman and will do as she pleases. Always has. Right now, I've got to get the store open and decide what I'm going to do about Ori."

"I thought you weren't going to get him out of jail this time." Oscar's hands went to unbuckle the seat belt that didn't exist in his father's old truck. He pulled on the stiff door handle and shoved a shoulder to the door to help it open. "So, what's left to do?"

"I'll give him time to think and come up with his own plan, then I'll go see him again. I'm not leaving Ori in there to punish him." Orville opened his door. "I'm leaving him in there to help him come to some decisions. Sometimes reaching the right option only happens when all the easy options are gone."

"What about..." Oscar's lips turned down. "What about Momma?"

"What about her?" Orville didn't look at Oscar. He slid from the seat and slammed the truck door closed, ending the conversation. She'd hurt him back then. Every letter that came saying she needed a few more months, every night sitting by the phone waiting for her to call when she didn't. No. She'd pushed and shoved, trying to get away from him and their kids, each letter getting further and further apart, until they quit coming. That wound, the dagger she'd shoved through his heart when she'd driven away, had healed, scabbed over, and grown a callous so thick that there was no worry of her ever hurting him again.

Orville looked back as Oscar disappeared down the sidewalk. She couldn't hurt him. He wouldn't let her in even if she wanted back in. She didn't, obviously, or she wouldn't have been hanging all over Gordon. Would she do right by the kids? They were grown, able to make their own decisions, but he was still their father... their protector.

Lucy popped a breath mint into her mouth and pulled her handbag up on her shoulder. Orville's truck was the only one in the lot besides hers. It was time to do this. She climbed out of the vehicle and hurried across the faded parking lot, stepping over a pothole full of yesterday's rainwater. The smell of fried food floated through the air from a nearby chicken place, and her stomach rumbled. She'd eat later, after she had this load off her chest. In the distance cheerleaders chanted in sing-song voices, probably practicing at the high school a few blocks away.

Lucy pulled open the door to the store, and the bell jingled above her head. She stood still, taking in the flood of memories that washed over her as her past came back to slap her in the face. The old Coke chest still sat over to the left. The thing had to be ancient, but if she lifted the lid, it would be stocked with Coke in the little bottles, so cold the liquid would sting your throat going down. Orville allowed the boys to have one every once in a while, as a special treat when they came with her to the store. The display case near the cash register, with glass so old it was tinted yellow, had a crack across the front covered by a piece of ancient duct tape. The crack nor the faded silver tape hadn't been there when she left. She walked down the aisle between the collections of bar stools, old chifferobes in need of refurnishing, crates of dusty vinyl records, and all the other "junk" toward the regis-ter, her shoes echoing on the worn pinewood floor. "Hello?" She hit the little bell near a plastic dog with a bobbling head. The sound echoed through the cavernous building. "Orville?"

"Hello, Lucy."

A shiver of heat washed down her back, and she pulled in a gulp of air. Orville had always been good looking. His broad shoulders, jet black hair, and eyes as blue as the sky in the summer, turned every woman's head when they were younger. Now his hair was peppered with gray, and his body was a little thinner. That voice—the one thing about him that had always been her undoing. It hadn't changed. Deep and gravely, and so masculine that it made her break out in goosebumps—it was still the same.

She tilted her chin up and turned. "Hello, Orville." She waited for him to speak again, but he stood there staring, his face calm, unemotional. *Okay. I can act like this is no big deal, too.* "I need to talk to you about signing the divorce papers."

"What did you do to your hair?"

Lucy shifted her purse on her shoulder. "I changed it. Last year." Her hand rose, and she fluffed the curls around her face. Would she ever get used to them? Chemo curls is what the nurse had called them. "Orville, we have to talk about the divorce papers."

"You're too thin." Orville's eyes roamed from Lucy's hand, pushing through her curls, down to her fuchsia pink toenails, then slowly back up to her face. "Looks like a puff of wind could knock you down."

Lucy reached down and tugged on her gauzy white peasant blouse, her jaw becoming hard. "Gordon seems to think I look alright."

"Gordon has been sniffing after you ever since you came to Red Creek when you were fifteen. I guess he finally caught you."

Lucy's eyes flashed. Why had she thought he would act reasonable, be an adult about this? She should have known better. "Look. I'm trying to be polite, but here's the deal. Gordon and I are getting married. I need you to sign the divorce papers so we can set a date and start planning the wedding."

"Are you moving back to Red Creek?" One corner of Orville's mouth crept up in a nonchalant smile. "For good?"

"Of course I'm moving back." Lucy's spine stiffened. "How else could I marry Gordon?"

"You've been married to me all these years and living in Nashville. I figured if ole Gordon wanted you bad enough, he would do like I've done and let his wife live wherever made her happy while he stayed home... out of her way."

Heat, a different kind of heat from a few minutes ago, crept up Lucy's neck. She reached into her purse, pulled out the envelope stuffed full of papers, and stuck it in his direction. "Sign the papers, Orville. You have to."

"It seems to me that since you have taken your own sweet time in coming home, that I can at least take a day or two to mull this over."

Lucy shoved her hand toward him again, but he didn't move, just continued to smile his smug smile. "Orville, it's time. Sign the papers." She waited, but he didn't move. "Fine." She threw the envelope on the floor at his feet. "I'll be back tomorrow. Sign them, Orville. Don't make me get a lawyer. They can be expensive."

"Not mine. You might have heard of him. Odysseus Robinson? I hear he's the best lawyer in town."

Lucy's eyes softened. "Odi's a lawyer? Little, shy Odi? I didn't know that."

"There's a lot you don't know, Lucy." The smile melted off of Orville's face and a stony stare took its place. "A whole lot."

"I'm not the woman I was when I left, Orville." Lucy blinked. She would not cry, would not let him see her break down. "I was wrong back then, but I'm back, and I've changed. I want to get to know my... our kids." Her voice became dull, the fight in her melting away. "Sign the papers, and I will leave you alone, but I plan on getting to know the children."

Orville continued to stare. Lucy's shoulders slumped. "Tomorrow, Orville. Sign the papers." She brushed past him and hurried from the store before the tears started. Why couldn't he do this the easy way? Why did he have to behave like... like a Robinson?

Chapter Three

L ucy waited for the bellboy to leave the room, then turned, taking in the extravagance. Gordon assured her that singing in the restaurant downstairs would be more than enough to cover her hotel room and meals, but was it? The billboard sitting at the entrance of the hotel restaurant downstairs barely resembled the woman she was now. The cancer and its treatment had done more than replace her board straight silvery-blond hair with strawberry curls that refused to be tamed. It had taken a piece of her, changed her, brought her so low that she had to accept help from the One she had been ignoring for years.

Gone was the woman who did everything in her power to hang on to her youth, her notoriety, and the small inkling of fame she had found as a country music singer. Singing about one-night stands, drinking, cheating, and wild living had never bothered her before. It was all an act, not the real woman she was, and she had played the part to sell the image. But now....

She looked at the reflection staring back at her in the gold-framed mirror above the cherry wood desk in the entryway of the luxury hotel suite. Would people want to listen to Lucy

Robinson play her acoustic guitar and sing the old songs about love and loss and family and heartache? Would they accept that she now threw in songs about her faith? Just her and the guitar without all the pomp and glitz that had been part of her trademark before? Only time would tell.

A knock sounded at the door, and she turned and opened it, needing a distraction from her worries. "Gordon, these are beautiful." She took the bouquet of yellow roses from the man she had pledged to marry and turned her cheek for him to kiss. "Come in and have a seat. I just walked through the door myself."

Gordon followed Lucy into the room and sat on the cream-colored leather sofa, watching her walk to the kitchen area to add water to the flowers. "How did it go with Orville? I started to call you, but decided to just drive over here and wait for you instead." His eyes scanned his surroundings, the gas fireplace on one wall, the floor to ceiling glass windows and sliding door leading to a private balcony overlooking the forest behind them, the double doors on the other side of the small kitchen area leading to the bedroom. "Do you think you will be comfortable enough here? You can come stay in the pool house at my place if this doesn't work out. Don't feel like you have to stay here if you don't like it."

"This is more than enough for me, Gordon, really." Lucy stepped back into the living area and sat on the couch beside him. "Back when I was opening for Cal Warren, I lived in the back corner of a tour bus for an entire year." She leaned back on the couch as a frown creased her brow. "I just hope people will actually want to come see and hear me—this new me — play and sing."

"You are Red Creek's hometown girl." Gordon leaned back on the couch and turned to face Lucy. "They are going to love you as much as I do. Trust me."

OUR HEAD STRONG LOVE

Lucy reached up and rubbed the tip of her ring finger along her lower lip. "I hope so."

"They will." Gordon reached over and patted her knee. "Don't worry. Now, tell me how it went with Orville? Can we set a date for the wedding?"

"No." Lucy sat forward and frustration flickered through her eyes. "I left the papers with him though. I'll give him a day or two to get his britches out of a wad, then I'll try again. He's just being so... stubborn, and for no reason."

"It had to be a shock. Seeing you again after all this time without any warning."

"I guess so, but he did tell me something good." Lucy's face softened. "Did you know Odi is a lawyer?" She rolled her eyes. "Of course you did. I forget you see my kids every week." She slipped her feet from her sandals and tucked them under her thighs, spreading her skirt around her on the couch. "Oscar's an accountant. Owen has a business degree, and you said he is working for you?"

"Yes, he started managing the hotel shortly after it opened."

"Odi is a lawyer and Olivia has the restaurant. That leaves Orion and Oliver. What are they doing?"

"Oliver is the boys' basketball coach at the school. They've gone to state for the past three years and won state last year. He's doing a phenomenal job with those kids."

"And Ori?" Lucy's smile faded. "Gordon, why are you looking like that? Is Orion okay? He's not sick or anything, is he?"

"No, last time I saw him, he was healthy as a horse."

"Then what?" Lucy raised her eyebrows. "Gordon Blue, tell me what's going on with my son?"

"He's in jail." Fear spread across Lucy's face and Gordon's brow creased. "Now don't get upset. From what I understand, it's just another little..."

17

"Another?" Lucy's eyes narrowed. "What's he doing? He's not a drug addict, is he?" Words spilled from Lucy's lips. "Gordon, I get that when I was having the chemo and the surgery you didn't talk about what was going on here with your son and my kids because you didn't want to upset me, but you better tell me what is going on with Ori—and tell me now."

"Now calm down, Lucy." Gordon leaned over and tried to pat her knee again, but her icy glare stopped him. "No." He pulled his hand back. "As far as I know, he doesn't have any drug habits. I can't see Orville letting him work for him and live with him if he was doing drugs."

"So?" Lucy raised her hands in frustrated annoyance. Sometimes Gordon was too calm, too easygoing. "Why is he in jail? Spit it out, or I'm going to wring it out of you."

"He got in a fight at a bar on the edge of the county, and the sheriff brought him in for disorderly conduct, or at least that's what I heard."

"Oh." Lucy leaned back against the couch again. "That's not too bad. I remember Orville got in a fight out at the gravel pit when we were dating, and the sheriff had to take him in and kept him overnight." Her eyes narrowed. "I guess Orville is taking care of it."

"I'm sure he is. He did before."

"Before?" Lucy stared at Gordon, concern and doubt dripping from the word. "Do you think I need to go check on him? I mean, it couldn't hurt anything, could it?"

"Orville's probably already bailed him out by now, Lucy. Why don't you just wait until tomorrow and see where things stand?" He sat forward and looked at his watch. "Besides, you have to get ready for your show tonight."

"Yeah." Lucy watched Gordon stand. "I guess if they've made it twenty-three years without my help, they can make it one more night."

"Dad." Early the next morning, Owen burst through the front door of the Robinson family home and headed to the dining room. He had been living with his father and working at his store until last year. This changed when he started managing the hotel. Shortly after, he had moved out to an apartment in town. That left Oscar, Oliver, and Ori at home. Owen still came and went in his father's house like he lived there, just like the rest of the kids. "Did you know that your wife—our mother—is in town?"

Orville stared up from his plate of bacon, biscuits, and scrambled eggs that Sadie had come over and cooked. He loved Sadie's homemade biscuits, but if she didn't stop nagging him about changing that light switch, he was going to start buying the biscuits in a can. "She came by the store yesterday. You should stop by and see me more often. Then I could tell you these sorts of things."

"You have a phone, Dad." Owen drug a chair out from the long wooden dining table, scarred from years and years of use. The table, as well as the house, had been Orville's father's and his grandfather's before him. "Why didn't you call and tell me? Mr. Blue had me set up a sound system to start having entertainment on the little stage area in the dining room, but he wouldn't tell me who he had booked. Now I know why."

"Have you talked to her?" Orville picked up his mug of coffee, black and steaming. "I'm surprised you recognized her. Your brother didn't."

"Which brother?" Owen sat down across from Orville and tore a biscuit from the pan in the middle of the table.

"Oscar. He saw her when we drove past the Blue building yesterday. By the way, did you hear that your brother's in jail again?"

"Yeah, I heard." Owen ripped a paper towel from the nearby roll laying on the table and laid it in front of him. No need to ask which brother this time. He popped open the biscuit and grabbed the jar of strawberry preserves in front of his father's plate. "But no, I didn't recognize her. Mr. Blue put a poster of her on a stand in the lobby yesterday, and I recognized her from the poster. In the poster she looks like that picture in the living room." He picked up the fork off of Orville's plate and scooped out a glob of jam from the sticky jar and smeared it on his biscuit. "She doesn't look like that poster now, though."

"No." Orville watched his son lick the fork, then stick it back on his plate. Undoubtably, he didn't act like that in the fancy hotel he ran. "Did she draw a crowd last night?"

"Yes, sir. The place was packed." Owen licked the ruby red jam dripping from the corner of the biscuit. "That's why I didn't get to talk to her. When she was done singing, people swarmed her like she was a queen bee." He took a bite of the biscuit and leaned back in the wooden dining chair. "Besides. I figured I'd talk to you first and see what you are planning on doing."

"Doing?" Orville took another drink of his coffee and stuck the last bite of bacon in his mouth.

"Yeah, Dad." Owen's eyes narrowed as he stared across the table. "She's been gone forever. Don't you think we need to— I don't know—find out why she's here?" His tongue darted out and licked a crumb from his lower lip. "Do Ollie and Olivia know she's here? Or Odi? Dad, this is just crazy."

"I haven't talked to your sister, so I don't know. She calls about as much as you do since she started getting that restaurant up and going." He scraped his chair across the old wooden floors, scooting away from the table. "I told Oliver this morning and I haven't spoken to Odi in a coon's age."

"What did Ollie say?"

"Not much." Orville stood. "You know your little brother. He's not going to say a whole lot until he's had a while to think about it."

"Yeah. Guess so." Owen stood. "You have any more coffee?"

"In the kitchen."

"So, what's the plan?" Owen shoved the last third of the biscuit in his mouth. He wiped his chin with the paper towel. "You gonna go talk to her and see what's going on?"

"She came and talked to me yesterday—like I said." Orville shoved his chair back under the table. Sadie would be by in a while to wash the dishes. Now that Olivia and her husband Quinn had moved out, his older sister came over most days and helped straighten up. He gave her a little money every month to help her make ends meet. Her little dab of retirement she drew from her dead husband didn't quite go far enough. He didn't ask her to come help him, but Sadie wouldn't take the money if she couldn't do something in return. She was sort of like him.

"What did she say?" Owen wadded the paper towel in his fist and tossed it on the table. "Is she here for good? Did she ask about us?"

"She said she's here for good. We didn't talk much. I was busy."

"Do you think we could all get together and invite her over, maybe Sunday? Ollie can make chicken pie and we can... I don't know. Talk to her."

"Y'all can do that if you want." Orville turned and started toward the living room. "Make sure you invite her fiancé, too. It would be impolite to leave him out."

21

"Fiancé?" Owen looked at his father's back, walking away. "Dad?"

Orville turned and looked at Owen. "I'm sure she'll tell you all about it when you talk to her. Make sure and tell me if she's coming on Sunday. If she is, I'll need to get your brother out of jail."

Chapter Four

L
ast night had been a success. Not only had the restaurant been full, the crowd welcomed her with open arms. Many people from Red Creek had followed her career over the past two decades and were delighted to see her back in town. Of course, everyone that knew her from before asked about Orville and the kids.

This morning, Lucy sipped her coffee and looked out the window to the woods behind the hotel. Since she had come to know the Lord last year, really know Him, she had started her days reading the Bible and just having a time to pray and think. A few things were made clear to her over the past few months, things that brought her back to Red Creek. One thing was, she needed to meet her kids and apologize for not being the mother to them that she should have been. Another was she needed to apologize to Orville for breaking her word to him over and over, and then, in the end, leaving him so she could pursue her dream of making it big as a singer.

When she had been alone in Nashville, writing in her journal and seeking God's guidance and peace, doing these things had seemed noble. Now, actually being in Red Creek, where all she had to do was drive down the street to talk to her family, the very idea of confronting them, confessing her sins to the ones she sinned against, laying herself open for their judgement, it all petrified her.

Knock, knock. She looked at the clock above the fireplace. Who in the world would be coming to visit her at eight-thirty in the morning? Gordon said last night that he would be busy all day and wouldn't see her again until tonight when she sang. Plus, he knew better than to bother her before ten, bless his heart. She pulled her robe around her, tied the belt snug, and walked to the door.

"Orville?" Lucy ran her fingers through the top of her head, her curls sticking out in every direction. The corners of his lips turned up slightly, and she quit fiddling with her hair. "Am I making it worse? It sticks out in every direction until I wet it."

"Let's just say that you're about a foot taller today than you were yesterday." He nodded toward the top of her head, and his mouth broke into a full grin. "Not everybody can pull off the Bozo look, but it's kind of cute on you."

"Bozo, huh?" Lucy laughed and shoved the door open. "Come on in, and I'll pour you some coffee. You still take it black?"

"Yeah." Orville followed her into the hotel room and waited while she poured his coffee. "This sure is a fancy room."

"It's very nice." Lucy stepped back into the living room area and handed Orville his cup. "Take a seat." She picked her open Bible up from the couch and laid it on the coffee table.

Orville sat down on one end of the long leather couch and watched as Lucy sat on the other, re-tucking her robe around her thin frame. "I need to talk to you. About our children."

Lucy leaned forward and picked up her half-empty cup of coffee. "Gordon told me that Ori is in jail." Lucy lifted the coffee cup to her lips and cut her eyes up at Orville. He still had a head full of hair, more gray now than black. Back in the day, he wore his jet-black curls just long enough to touch the collar of his shirt, just long enough to curl around her fingers when she ran her hands through it.

"I'm taking care of that." Orville took a sip of the coffee and winced. He set the cup on the table beside him. "Owen saw you last night. He said you packed the house."

"He was here?" Lucy set her cup down beside Orville's. "I know he works here, but I didn't see him last night. Is he still as hyper as he used to be?"

"Almost, but he controls it pretty good. He said there were too many people around to come talk to you, but he was pretty worked up this morning about you being here."

"I imagine they all will be." Lucy's shoulders sagged. "Do they hate me, Orville?"

"No, I don't think so. I haven't talked to Odi, Ori, or Olivia yet, but the other three were confused about you showing up out of the blue, maybe a little aggravated, but not angry, at least not in a hateful way."

"I wouldn't blame them if they were."

"That's what I want to talk to you about." Orville reached into his pocket and pulled out a piece of peppermint. "This morning, Owen said he was going to get with the others and have them all come to the house on Sunday. He's going to come by here sometime today and invite you to Sunday dinner so they can figure out where you stand... with them."

"Are you okay with that?" Lucy watched Orville unwrap the candy and put it in his mouth. When had he given up smoking? "I want to talk with them, try to explain a few things, but if you want me to wait until after the divorce goes through, I will."

"Well." Orville's eyes met Lucy's. "Here's what I came to say. Those kids are my life. They may be grown, but they're still my young'uns. I'm still their father, and I take that very serious."

"Okay." Lucy held his gaze, holding her breath for what he was about to say. Could he convince the kids to not see her? Would he do that?

"Until I see how things pan out... with you and them, I'm going to just hold on to the divorce papers."

"Hold on to them?" Lucy's jaw tightened. "Why? For how long?"

"That depends on you, I guess. You get to know them, treat them right, really stick around and act like... well, like a mother should, then I'll sign your papers, and we'll be done." He leaned forward, his eyes cutting into hers. "But if you hurt my kids, Lucy, I promise you one thing. I'll make sure you are never free of me."

"Now you listen here, Orville Robinson." Lucy leaned forward, her nose inches from him, so close she could smell the spicy scent of his aftershave. "Those kids are my kids, too. I am here to set things straight with them, and I will." A curl flopped down in front of her eyes, and she jerked her head, tossing it out of her line of vision. "But you have no right to hold the divorce papers over my head."

"Right?" Orville smirked, his voice calm. "We can talk about right if you really want to, Lucy. Like who was right when you left, abandoning us, promising to be back in six months, to come home every month to visit, but never did. Like who was right to quit answering my phone calls when I was calling to find out when you were coming to spend time with *your* kids? Do you really want to talk about right?"

Heat flushed Lucy's chest and ran up her neck. "Are you finished? Because I need to get a shower and get dressed."

"I'm finished." Orville stood. "Don't hurt our kids, Lucy. You can't hurt me, and I won't let you hurt them."

"I won't." She stood and glanced down at the open Bible

laying between their coffee cups. "I'm not the woman I was back then."

"Talk's cheap, Lucy. Time will tell."

He was right. That didn't make it hurt a bit less though. He walked to the door, and tears filled her eyes. He didn't look back, didn't say goodbye, just walked out. She sat there, the battle to give in to the anger raging against the justification of his words. He was telling the truth. She had left him—and their children high and dry. But abandon? That didn't seem fair. They had agreed that she should go, try to make a go of her career, get it out of her system. When he called, and she told him she was so close to making a breakthrough, he had agreed that she should keep going. He even said he understood she couldn't make it home for a visit right then. He'd agreed... at least at first. But had he really? Had she given him any other option when she refused to come home?

She stood and raked the tears from her face. No, no feeling sorry for herself. Being a go-getter and wanting it all had gotten her into this mess. Being a go-getter and wanting it all would get her out. *Lord, I know he has a right to be angry, a right to protect our kids. Lord, help me find a way to break through his shell and show him I'm not who I was.*

Her phone buzzed, and she looked at the screen. Gordon. She couldn't talk to him right now. Not when her mind was so scrambled. She would call him later, when she was a little more together. She went to the bedroom and pulled out a pair of jeans and a white eyelet blouse. She laid the clothes on the bed and bit her lower lip. Did that look motherly enough? She hung up the jeans and pulled out a denim knee-length skirt. Better. She stepped into the bathroom and turned on the shower. First, she would go downstairs and find out if Owen was around. Give him an opportunity to invite her over Sunday, like Orville said he was planning on doing. She would then go see if Ori was still in jail. If he was, she would get him out. If the sheriff wouldn't cooperate, Gordon would have to pull a few strings and make it happen. That would be a good start to showing Orville that she had changed. He obviously couldn't get their son out, or he would have. She would help.

Would she have time to see the twins after that? She'd never sprung anyone from the pokey before. It might take all day. Then there were Oscar and Odi. She climbed into the shower and scrubbed her hair with a vengeance, the hot water pounding against her skin as memories of the day she left all those years before cascaded through her mind. Eight-year-old Oscar had hugged her neck and given her a picture he had drawn of the family... so she wouldn't forget them. When six-year-old Owen and five-year-old Ori started crying, not wanting to let her go, Oscar had taken their hands, pulling them back, while Orville held the three-year-old twins in his arms. Four-year-old Odi wrapped his thin little arms around his father's leg, thumb stuck securely in his mouth. "Momma won't be gone long," her eight-year-old had explained to his siblings. "Y'all let her go."

Those words from her oldest child had haunted her for years. Until she'd somehow convinced herself that what she had done was okay... for everyone.

When she found the lump and started the cancer treatments, when she needed someone, no one was there. No one —except God. She had run away from everyone, but God was still there. She stared down at the puckered pink scar across the right side of her rib cage. Cancer had taken so much, but it had given as well. Given her a relationship with her Father. He'd gotten her through the cancer, but the lies she'd allowed herself to believe, the words that let her off the hook for what she had done to her family, no longer worked. Coming to God meant coming clean, being truthful not only with Him, but with herself. It had not been pretty, but it had been the first step in making things right.

She stepped out of the shower and finished getting ready. A few minutes later she opened her hotel room door, and the soft whoosh of the elevator opening came from down the hall. She stuck her key card in her purse and looked up as a young man with coal-black hair and the same piercing blue eyes as Orville approached. His shoulders were broader than his father's, or maybe it was just because he was younger and more muscular, but there was no doubt this was one of her sons. "Owen?"

"Guess again."

A knot tightened in Lucy's gut. "Oscar?"

"That's right." Oscar's eyes, cold as steel, stared at his mother. "For a minute there, I thought you might have forgotten who I was... Mother."

Chapter Five

The nostalgic smell of the antique records in their old cardboard covers wafted into Orville's nose as he dug through the box of forty-fives. Before Owen went to work at the Blue Hotel, he set up a website for the junk business. Orville hadn't been on board with the idea, but at the time, Owen assured him he and Ori would handle the site and all on-line orders and inquiries. Now, as was often the way with things, his sons were not around, and they left Orville to keep their promises.

The bell above the door jingled, cutting into his quiet brooding. "Anybody manning the ship?" Sadie's voice floated across the inventory of old bedroom furniture, display cases for forgotten toys, every kind of glassware imaginable, along with books, records, knick-knacks, and too many other large and small items Orville had rounded up over the years. He would eventually re-home his finds to a collector or whimsical soul who liked to think outside the box... or at least, that was the plan.

"Back here." Orville pulled out an Elvis album, *GI Blues*, from a milk crate full of records. A young Elvis Presley in a brown service uniform stared at him through the layer of dust clinging to the plastic, keeping the actual record jacket in pristine condition. He wiped the cover against the side of his hip and added it to the six others he'd found. He swiped his dusty fingers across his pants leg and watched Sadie weave through the merchandise, walking toward him. "Owen texted. Somebody is wanting all the Elvis records we have. Since Ori is not here, I'm doing his job."

"It doesn't seem to be hurting you any." Sadie thumbed through the stack of records Orville was building and pulled out the one with Elvis in his infamous white sequined jumpsuit. "That was a gorgeous man."

"If you say so." Orville started toward the front of the store. "Bring those with you." He'd left Lucy earlier that day and hadn't been in the mood to chit chat since their conversation. When she talked about their children, she'd seemed so sincere in her plans of becoming a part of their lives. He patted his shirt pocket. Out of peppermint. He'd run by the dollar store on the way home and grab a new bag.

He stepped over to the ancient drink box, the refrigerator motor humming. The lid squeaked horribly as he pulled it open, but the Coke he pulled out was ice cold. "Want one?" He glanced back at his older sister.

"No. I had a glass of tea on the way over." She watched him pop the metal drink lid on the old-timey bottle opener on the side of the box, then followed him to the counter. "Where do you want these?"

"Just lay them back there out of the way. Owen or Ori will have to mail them. I told them I wasn't interested in doing online business. They can take it from here."

"They're trying to help, Orville. You know they're worried about you and this place going under." She set the records down on a wobbly barstool shoved in the corner behind her. "Why don't you tell them? Set their minds at ease?"

"I have my reasons." Orville tilted the little drink bottle to his lips and sipped just enough of the icy liquid to burn his throat on the way down. He loved his sister. She had stepped in when Lucy left all those years ago and filled in the gap as best she could, especially with Olivia. She had been more of a momma than an aunt to his kids, and he loved her for it. Since she gave her heart so freely to his family, she also felt she had the right to give her advice and opinions just as freely. Usually they rolled off Orville like water off a duck's back. He could tune her out and go on about his business. Today, though, today he needed quiet. Time to settle his brain around Lucy and what her reappearance would mean to his family.

"Is it true what I heard at the post office?"

"Stamps going up again? Yeah, probably."

"Smart alec." Sadie stepped up to the counter beside Orville and started straightening the different piles of papers, tossing old peppermint wrappers in the trash can at their feet. "No. Is it true that Lucy is back in town?"

"Yeah." Orville reached up and absently patted his empty pocket again. "She's staying at the Blue Hotel."

Sadie laid her tanned and calloused hand on Orville's back. She worked almost as hard as he did, hoeing the corn and peas and other vegetables in their shared garden. "What are you going to do? Have you talked to the kids about her?"

"She's coming to the house after church Sunday for dinner." Orville picked up the six ounce Coke bottle and tilted his head back, downing the rest of the drink in three gulps, before slamming the bottle back on the counter.

"Are you sure that's such a good idea?" Sadie's brow furrowed. "Sounds like you're inviting trouble. You know how she hurt you and the kids before."

"I didn't invite anybody." Orville pulled in a heavy breath. "Owen's setting it up. I'm just the father, the man that raised them, and happens to own the house and this store." He picked the bottle up and stepped around the counter, away from Sadie. "But seems like my kids are too old to let me handle my own affairs."

"Lucy's their mother, Orville." Sadie watched her little brother, her mouth pinching. "This whole affair is as much their business as it is yours. Probably more. You can wash your hands of her—sign those infernal divorce papers you've kept hidden away for all these years and be done with it. But your kids." Her voice softened. "They've always wondered why she left, what was more important to her than them. Now that she's back, I imagine they will make it their business to find out." She picked up a stack of mail and tapped it against the counter. "At least some of them will. Maybe having her over to your house where you can... monitor what she tells them. Maybe that will be best."

"Best or not, that's what they have planned. And don't worry about the divorce papers. She brought her own set." He set the empty Coke bottle in the wooden crate near a lot of Coca-Cola memorabilia. "Why are you here?" He turned and stared at his sister. Had she come by to be nosey? Probably. Either way, he was tired of talking and needed to go check on Ori.

Sadie shrugged her shoulders, Orville's grumpy tone not bothering her in the least. "I came by to tell you that the watermelons are ready to pick. I've gotten Oliver and some of his basketball players to pick them and load them. I'm going to sell them off the tailgate of the truck between the Blue Hotel and Olivia's place." She stepped around the counter and followed Orville back toward the door. "I came by to check and see if you wanted to put a few in front of the store to sell."

"That's fine." Orville stopped at the door to the store and turned, Sadie almost bumping into him. "It's gonna be awful hot sitting on the side of the road. When are you going out there?"

"Oliver has the boys picking them and loading the truck now." She nodded her head toward the sidewalk out front. "That's why I'm in his truck. I'm leaving here and going back to swap with him. I should be able to get set up before everybody is getting off work this evening, even with dropping back by here to leave you a few."

"Do you want me to sell the watermelons, and you cover the store?" Orville rubbed his hand across his jaw. He needed to go ahead and bail Ori out of jail. The last thing he needed was his gray-haired sister having a heat stroke from selling watermelons in the mid-day sun. Ori was young and healthy. He could do that and hopefully keep out of trouble.

"No." Sadie smiled up at Orville. "Don't you worry about me. I've got an umbrella and a little battery-operated fan and a cooler full of iced tea. If it gets too hot, I'll just crank the truck and sit in the A.C. This isn't my first rodeo, you know." She walked around her brother and opened the front door, the bell jingling as she stepped through. "You've got enough on your plate without me. I didn't get to be this age by being stupid, you know."

Orville took his time locking the store door, giving his sister time to drive away so he wouldn't have to talk anymore. He drove home and walked through the empty house, flipping the light in his bedroom. It flickered a couple of times before coming on. He'd have to check on that. Another thing to put on his list. His knees popped as he dropped to the floor and lifted the bedspread. His arm reached under and fished out the ancient black metal box. He pulled out enough money from the box to pay Ori's bail, slammed the squeaky lid, and slid it back toward the far corner near the wall, too far for his sister or daughter to find when they took it upon themselves to clean his room.

His truck drove down his bumpy driveway, dodging the cavernous mudholes washed out by the frequent rains. It had been a wet spring. He needed to get a load of gravel out here and fill in all these holes. There was always something to worry about, something to fix, or pay somebody else to fix. He passed the garden spot and honked his horn as Oliver, along with ten teenage boys, carried enormous green watermelons from their garden to Sadie's pickup. Sadie stood at the back of the truck, pointing this way and that, no doubt giving orders like a drill sergeant. They all looked in his direction as he stuck his arm out the window and waved. Yeah, his place needed a lot of work, but it was his place. A place for his family to come to and know they were home.

A few minutes later, he drove through town and pulled into a park in front of the sheriff's office, the bail money neatly folded in his front pocket. "JT." Orville blinked as his eyes adjusted to the dim yellow light from the long fluorescent bulbs above his head. If he worked here, he would put in brighter lighting. He stepped across the empty room and pounded his fist on the desk. "JT?" The place didn't have a secretary, and JT nor the deputy were ever in the front.

"Hold your horses, Orville." JT stepped out of his office, wiping his mouth with a white paper napkin. "I'm trying to wolf down my lunch before supper time. Sometimes this place is like Grand Central Station."

"I'm here to pay Ori's bail." Orville didn't bother being social. It was the jail house after all. "This won't take but a minute, then you can get back to stuffing your face."

"Ori's not here." JT looked at the money in Orville's hand, then back at his face. "I figured you knew."

A small knot curled in Orville's stomach. "What do you mean, he's not here? What did you do with my boy, JT?" Orville's hand curled into a fist around the money in his palm. "So help me if you..."

"Calm down, Orville." JT raised his hand up like a shield. "I haven't done anything with your boy. You're gonna start

35

having chest pain and have the whole Robinson clan down on my head."

"No, I'm not." Orville clenched his jaw and shoved the fist full of money into his pants pocket. "A man has one minor episode of chest pain, and everyone decides he's old and decrepit. That was a one time thing. Besides, the doctor said it was a stomach ulcer, not my heart at all." He placed both palms on the desk between him and the sheriff and leaned forward. "Tell me what you've done with my boy, or I'm going to show you just how strong my heart and the rest of me still is."

"Lucy Robinson bailed Ori out about thirty minutes ago, Orville." JT took a step backwards and held both hands up in surrender. "I haven't done anything with your kid. I figured Ori or your wife would have already called and told you."

"Lucy?" Orville's eyebrows raised. "Bailed out Ori?"

"Yeah. That's what I just said." JT lowered his hands. "Ori didn't even know who she was at first, but she talked with him a few minutes before they left—together." JT watched Orville's scowl deepen. "He's a grown man, Orville, like you said. And she is his mother."

Orville turned and walked out of the sheriff's office, not answering JT. The heat and bright sunlight slammed into him as he crossed the sidewalk and got back in his truck. What game was she playing? Was she trying to win Ori over by paying his bail?

He pulled out from in front of the jailhouse and started back to his store. The parking lot was empty, but the lights were on inside. The door jingled as he walked through the unlocked door he had locked a couple of hours ago when he left.

"Hey, Pop." Ori looked up from where he stood behind the counter, flipping through the Elvis records. "I saw the email from the customer requesting these. I think there's a few more in that box in the back. I'll get these in the mail tomorrow."

"Good." Orville pulled his brow low. "How did you get out of jail?"

"You wouldn't believe me if I told you."

Chapter Six

O rville stepped in the back door of the church house and eased down the aisle. One of the men from his Sunday school class had stopped him outside to discuss replacing the wooden steps on an elderly couple's front porch. The couple, being in their eighties, were on a fixed income and couldn't afford to have the steps fixed. Either the old man or his wife was going to break a hip if the church didn't do something soon. Their conversation led to a plan to buy the lumber out of the helping hands fund from the men's class that Orville oversaw. They would get a crew of volunteers together Wednesday morning to build the couple a new set of steps, complete with new handrails.

He didn't mind coming in a few minutes late for preaching when being a good neighbor was the cause. The piano played "Holy, Holy, Holy" as he eased down the center aisle to the third row from the back on the right-hand side—the Robinson row. When all the crew were there, including Sadie, and a couple of their elderly aunts, they took up two rows, but everyone knew Orville sat on the third row on the outer edge.

The choir filed in from a side door near the front of the church and filled the chairs behind the podium as Orville stepped into the pew beside Quinn, his only son-in-law. Orville bowed his head, sending up a prayer for the preacher's words to penetrate his heart and for the music to lead him to truly worship. The piano continued, and the choir started to sing.

A shuffling sounded beside him, but he kept his head bowed, focusing on the reason he was there. Something sharp bumped him in his ribs, but he pressed his lips together. He'd have to have a talk with Quinn after church about respecting the worship time.

"Dad." Olivia's voice hissed into Orville's ear.

Orville opened one eye and looked down at his daughter, who apparently just traded places with her husband to get beside him. He scowled before pushing his eyes closed again. She knew better than to talk in church.

"Dad. Look."

The choir's song came to an end, and Orville lifted his head as everyone sat in unison from decades of practiced tradition. He glared at his only daughter, who scowled right back, not intimidated at all. She tilted her head toward the choir loft and stretched her gray eyes wide. Orville poked his lips together and turned to look at whatever she was insisting he needed to see. Had the preacher grown a second head? "Well... I'll be." The words rumbled from his chest before he could stop them. He coughed, trying to cover his outspoken blunder. His daughter snickered beside him, but he refused to look her way.

He set his jaw and looked back at the choir where Lucy sat, wearing one of the church's white choir robes, like she had been singing soprano for Jesus all along. Not singing songs about getting drunk and fooling around on your spouse and all the other lyrics that once led her toward the fame she craved over the years.

The choir director, a friend of Owen's who spent several nights at Orville's house through the kid's school years, read the church announcements. He then encouraged everyone to stand again and sing "Blessed Assurance." Orville stood, flipping to the page in the hymnal, and stared down at the book, not bothering to read the words he had known by heart since childhood. He listened, tuning his ear to Lucy's strong voice, her clear tone carrying through, leading the rest of the surrounding voices effortlessly without trying.

She had not sung in the choir when they were young. They married the week she turned eighteen, since she no longer needed her parents' permission. He had been twenty-three and practically robbed the cradle, but Lucy had climbed out of that cradle with only a little encouragement from Orville.

The next year, Oscar was born. Lucy quit her job at the factory, and for the following eight years, the Robinson brood grew steadily, rounding out to a nice even six when the twins came along. On a good Sunday, the kids all made it to church with their shoes on and their faces clean. On an average Sunday, they just made it to church. Suddenly, after eight years and six kids, Lucy left. Had she wanted to sing in the choir back then?

The song finished, and Orville sat back down with everyone else, not looking up to where Lucy sat, almost directly behind the preacher. Olivia's slender hand eased across and found his as he was pulling it back to his lap. He turned his face, head still down, and looked at her, his only daughter who looked so much like the woman in the choir.

"Love you, Daddy," Olivia whispered.

The preacher started praying, and Orville squeezed his daughter's hand. *Lord, I don't know what Lucy has planned. I can't see her heart, I know, but I know she's hurt us in the past. Lord, please don't let her hurt my children again.* He swallowed the lump trying to form in his throat. *And, Lord, help me see the truth where she's concerned. Not only what I want to see, nor what she wants me to see. Please, God, give me discernment about my wife.* He looked up as the preacher continued to pray and stared at Lucy, eyes squeezed shut, face tilted upward, a single tear running down her face.

That had gone surprisingly well. Lucy had met with the pastor of the church that Gordon attended on Saturday afternoon. Gordon had not thought that was necessary, but Lucy remembered enough about Red Creek to understand that gossip often weighed as heavy in the air as the sticky, hot humidity. "No, Gordon, I at least want the preacher to know my heart, and that I'm sincere in my plans. That way, when the rumors start flying, he won't have to try to figure out anything."

"Honey, I think you aren't giving everyone enough credit." Gordon had listened, watching Lucy tie a scarf around her head in front of the mirror. "You see how the people love you at the restaurant."

"Well, I'm not taking any chances. Someone will eventually remember those pictures in the tabloids from a decade ago where I was accused of breaking up Cal Warren's marriage. I'm still new in town, but eventually, all the hogwash from my past is going to surface." Lucy adjusted the scarf, pulling the curls back from her face one last time, and turned toward Gordon. "Most of it's a pack of lies, but that's not the point, anyway. The point is, I've changed, and I need a second chance. The Lord has forgiven me, so I figure the preacher will understand my circumstances better than most since he's a preacher... and as you said, has a little bit of a past of his own."

The visit with the preacher had gone well. He had introduced her to the song director that morning before church, who was thrilled to have her in the choir. The younger man didn't question her sincerity at all and had set the tone for the choir members. She remembered a lot of them from before. Everyone assumed she and Orville were divorced. She was certain a lot of them had negative feelings about a woman leaving six small children behind to pursue a singing career, but they didn't let them surface in the ten minutes while she slipped on her choir robe and took her spot with the sopranos on the front row. Thank goodness for that.

She'd spotted the Robinson bunch as soon as she entered the church in their usual spot near the back. Another thing that never changed. Olivia had smiled warmly at her, while Oliver's smile was more reserved. Ori had given her a lopsided grin and a thumbs up, and Owen had nodded at her. All of that was promising.

She scanned the church but didn't see Odi. At least she didn't think she saw Odi. After all, she hadn't seen him in twenty-three years. She had recognized the rest of the children. Well, at least she'd recognized them as being Robinsons, even if she wasn't sure which Robinson. Her eyes returned to the Robinson pews. Oscar sat on the row behind Olivia and the other siblings, next to Sadie. She caught his eye and smiled, but Oscar's look remained impassive. At least that was better than the coolness he'd offered in her hallway the other morning when he practically told her she wasn't wanted or needed in Red Creek. Oscar was definitely more skeptical of her intentions than his siblings.

The choir director stepped in front of them, and Lucy started singing the opening hymn along with the rest of the group, letting the words of praise wash over her. She was at church to worship, not scope out her family. Her voice blended with the others, and she smiled. She had very little to offer God, but she could give him her voice.

As they finished the last verse of the worship hymn, her eyes drifted from the church rafters back down to the congregation, down to where Orville's head was bowed, waiting for the prayer to begin. He must have slipped in during the song. She tried to focus on why she was there, but her eyes refused to go anywhere else. *Look up, Orville. Just look up so I can see your face, see what you are thinking.* She finally pulled her eyes away. It didn't matter as much if he didn't forgive her. What mattered was the children, restoring the relationship with them. Orville was as hardheaded as a brickbat, but he wasn't a mean man. Once he believed she had changed, that she truly only wanted to be a part of their children's lives, he would give her the divorce, and she could move on.

The preacher's voice filled the building, and Lucy tried to focus on what he was saying. The words *new mercies* filled her ears. She looked down again to the Robinson pew, but Orville's head remained down. If she really didn't care... if it really didn't matter whether he forgave her or not, why was her heart squeezing right now? She closed her eyes, tilting her chin up as a tear trickled down her cheek. *It's just because I have a history with him. That's all. And he's the father of my children. It's only natural to want to mend the fences with him.*

A day long ago flashed through her thoughts. Her stomach was so big with pregnancy that she couldn't get up from a chair without help. Orville had brought home a pack of M&M's and told five-year-old Oscar to divide them evenly among him and his three little brothers, all playing on the floor at her feet.

"You're ruining their supper." Lucy had leaned forward from the rocker and kissed Orville's warm lips. "Why don't you help me up, and let's feed them before they have the candy?"

"A little candy won't stop them from eating their meal." Orville had disappeared in the other room and returned a few minutes later with the Jergens lotion from the bathroom sink. "Besides, I still owe you a foot rub from last night." He sat down on the wooden floor at her feet and slipped off the worn baby blue house slippers. Orville had promised her a foot massage the night before, but she had fallen asleep while he was tucking Owen back in bed for the third time, which was not an unusual thing.

Another tear slipped down Lucy's cheek. The memory of Orville, muscular and oh so handsome with that five o'clock shadow and black wavy hair, sitting on the floor, singing her a love song, rubbing her feet, while the boys climbed all over her, flooded her mind and her heart. How had she ever, ever thought that fame and money were more important than the love of her husband and children?

She reached up and pressed her hands under her eyes as the preacher stepped away from the podium and the song leader returned. She stood to sing another hymn, but her throat was thick with remorse. *I can't go back. Lord, I know you've forgiven me, and I am desperately trying to forgive myself. It would be a whole lot easier to do that if Orville would find a way to forgive me, too.* She looked out at the congregation again as the church sang "Have Faith In God."

Orville's lips barely moved as he sang the song, his eyes staring toward the front, but not at her. She strained her ears, but could not hear his voice, his deep baritone, one of a kind voice, that was so prevalent in her memory a few seconds ago. No, he needed to forgive her. She would make him forgive her. Somehow.

Chapter Seven

Lucy's truck bounced from one pothole to the next, easing down the long gravel driveway to the Robinson home tucked into the woods a few miles outside of Red Creek. She slowed even more, looking at the enormous garden to the left, behind the barbwire fence in the clearing that had been nothing but trees when she moved away. Long neat rows of cornstalks, next to more rows of green plants, stood proudly in the Alabama sunshine. She recognized the rows of pole beans and black-eyed peas, but there were other things she wasn't sure about.

Her family moved to Red Creek from Birmingham when she was fifteen and had always lived in a suburb. Some years her daddy would till up a single six-foot row in their little backyard for a few tomato plants and a couple of squash, but that had been as close to gardening as she had gotten. Her daddy worked at the bank, and they'd settled into Red Creek life well enough. Three years later, she'd ran off and married Orville, definitely not the man her father had in mind for his only daughter. Her mother was a little more understanding, but neither had understood why she picked Orville over

Gordon Blue. Gordon, the baseball captain, was headed to college to make something of himself. Gordon had been head over heels in love with her from day one.

Gordon had introduced her to Orville, his older friend who was kind of quiet and worked for Gordon's father down at the garment factory. Gordon had been furious when she'd broken up with him a few months later. When he found out she was secretly seeing Orville, he had been crushed. Gordon never stayed mad long, though, and soon all three of them were friends again.

She and Gordon eventually graduated high school. He'd gone off to college, and she'd eloped with Orville. When Gordon moved home four years later with a new wife, the friends had grown apart. Sweet Gordon. When she needed money to follow her dream, he'd given it to her. Enough to get to Nashville and survive a few days until she could find a job, no strings attached. Eventually, he'd done a lot more. He hadn't understood her running away from her family either, not really, but he'd been there for her when she thought following her dream was what she needed to do.

Lucy pulled into the Robinson yard, surrounded by overgrown azalea bushes, redbud trees, magnolias, and oak and pines behind the house in the distance. She remembered the grass had always needed to be mowed with the dinky little push mower, but not today. The old metal rail fence, orange with rust, still closed in the spacious yard where a few chickens mingled around in the neatly trimmed grass. Several trucks were parked outside of the fence, and she pulled hers in among them. Only Orville's ancient pickup had crossed the cattle gap opening of the fence and actually parked in the yard in front of the house. She looked at the wrap-around porch littered with what looked like a vehicle motor, a pile of deer antlers, and several five gallon buckets scattered around between lawn chairs and folding metal chairs. If any home ever needed a woman's touch, it was this one.

She pulled her shades from her face and hung them on the visor, her eyes scanning the yard. The front door opened as she stepped from her truck. Olivia, her beautiful daughter, walked onto the porch, followed closely by Quinn Lewis, her husband. Lucy met him briefly yesterday at their restaurant. The handsome young man, with his friendly Louisiana accent, obviously adored Ollie. He stood in the doorway, holding open the screen door as Olivia made her way down the steps to meet Lucy.

The smell of freshly mowed grass, wisteria, honeysuckle, and country life in general, mixed with something else from inside the house. Home cooking. "Whatever you have planned for lunch smells amazing," Lucy called, strolling across the cattle gap and into the Robinson yard. A proud red rooster with a few bluish black tail feathers streaming high and mighty in an arc behind him, pranced across her path. She stopped, giving him the right of way. A dog, some mixture of hound, eased out from beneath a dust pile under the porch. It let out a long mournful howl, announcing Lucy's return.

"Hush, Bubba." Olivia shook her finger at the dog as she hurried toward her mother. "That's chicken pie, creamed corn, turnip greens, cornbread, and sliced tomatoes. It's not fancy, but it's Daddy's favorite, and the vegetables are fresh from the garden."

"That all sounds heavenly." Lucy stretched her hands out and grasped Olivia's as she approached. Her daughter had welcomed her in what appeared to be genuine warmth yesterday. She had dropped by the couple's restaurant unannounced and received the grand tour. They were scheduled to open the place some time soon and were neck deep in preparations. Sadie had also been there, helping Ollie in the kitchen. Her welcome had been polite, but a little more reserved. Lucy didn't blame her. How could she? She left the woman with a broken-hearted little brother, five young nephews, and a niece to care for while she drove away to follow a dream. The woman had only been married a few years herself back then, being a late bloomer, but Lucy hadn't thought about how her leaving would affect her sister-in-law. She hadn't been thinking about anyone but herself.

Ollie took Lucy's thin hands in hers and pulled her mother close into a tight hug. "You have no idea how happy I am that you're here." She stepped back and smiled, her eyes sparkling with dampness. "Everyone is inside." She looked over Lucy's shoulder toward her truck. "Where's Gordon? Owen said he'd be coming with you."

Orville stepped into the living room and sat down in his recliner. Laughter and chatter floated from the other room. He had to hand it to her. She was winning them over already. Even Odi, the skeptic who never showed up for family things, and when he was around, never engaged, was laughing and talking. Not just with Lucy, either. He'd actually picked at Ori about giving a little free legal advice if he ever decided to make his incarcerations a more permanent thing. The only one who put up a wall was Oscar, who'd obviously rather been fishing. He, like Orville, had eaten in silence, only speaking to answer direct questions.

A burst of laughter came from the kitchen, as miraculously, most of his sons had offered to help straighten up after the meal, so everyone could spend time together. Orville leaned his head back on the worn leather head rest where he had weathered so many storms in the past. His eyes narrowed. Is this what it could have—should have been like for all these years?

"There you are." Lucy stepped into the living room, her face glowing with cheerfulness. The rest of the family, minus Oscar, filed in behind her, spilling onto the furniture.

"It was a little crowded in the kitchen with all the help." Orville raised an eyebrow in the general direction where most of his sons had scattered. "I decided to wait for y'all in here."

"This has always been my favorite room of the house." Lucy stepped over to the ancient black upright piano, her fingers trailing silently over the yellowed keys. She gazed at her portrait of the woman she'd been when she left, hanging above it, and pulled in a deep breath. "Everything looks just like it did the last time I was here."

An awkward silence crept into the room, and Orville waited. This is what he was dreading, the hashing up of all their old garbage. "Yeah. You know I never have been one for change."

Lucy picked up the six string Gibson guitar propped against the piano and walked over to where Orville sat, watching her like a hawk, keeping an eye on his prey. "Play something, Orville." She stuck the acoustic guitar in his direction. Orville didn't reach out his hand as all the eyes watched him.

"Dad doesn't play, uh... Momma." Olivia smiled from the couch and nodded to her brother sitting in a dining room chair he brought along with him to the room. "Ori plays your guitar, and he's pretty good. I've tried to play your mandolin, but I sort of sound like a drowning cat."

Lucy's brow raised. She looked from Olivia back to Orville, her head tilting to the side. "What's she talking about?" She laid the guitar in Orville's lap and stepped over to the couch, squeezing in between Olivia and Oliver. "Honey, that's your daddy's guitar and mandolin." Her eyes scanned the room. "And I bet there's a fiddle tucked in a corner somewhere around here." She looked back at Orville and smiled. "Who do you think taught me how to play in the first place?"

"What?" Ori dragged the word out into more of an accusation than a question. "I don't ever remember Daddy touching any of those instruments." His head darted around the room. "Where's Oscar? Oscar!" Ori bellowed his brother's name into the air and waited, looking toward the dining room along with the rest of his family. Oscar stepped into the doorway and propped his shoulder against the frame, slowly bringing his glass of tea to his lips. "You ever remember Daddy playing the guitar or the mandolin?" Ori asked.

"He also plays the piano and the banjo and harmonica," Lucy said, acting like the revelation of Orville's musical talent was no big deal.

"Seems like I remember him playing years ago," Oscar said, his voice lacking the camaraderie the rest of the siblings were sharing. "Maybe, but that was back when I was small." He turned his cool stare to Lucy. "Right after you left us."

Orville picked the guitar up from his lap, taking in the pained expression flickering through Lucy's eyes. "Ori, you got a pick?"

"So, you can play?" Ori stepped over and handed Orville a guitar pick he retrieved from the top of the piano. "Well, I'll be."

Orville ignored Ori, grinning like a banshee as he handed him the pick. He strummed a few chords, adjusted a couple of the knobs on the end of the instrument, and strummed a few more chords. The guitar felt like a long-lost friend in his hands. Someone he'd ignored for far too long. He picked out the melody of Amazing Grace, adding a few runs here and there as he got lost in the music. After a couple of seconds, he opened his eyes and looked around the room.

Ori was still grinning, but the rest of the kids were staring at him like he had grown a set of antlers in the last three seconds. All the kids except Oscar as he had disappeared again.

"Dad." Olivia's eyes stretched wide. "Why didn't you let us know you could play? You are good, Dad."

"Oh, that's nothing." Lucy reached up and wiped her misty eyes. "You should hear him on the fiddle. That's where he really shines."

Orville looked down at the guitar, avoiding Olivia's questioning look and Lucy's tender gaze.

"Dad?" Olivia was not used to being ignored. "Do you have a fiddle somewhere?"

"No." Orville lifted the guitar from his lap and propped it against his knee. "I... broke it... a long time ago." The memory of that day flooded Orville's mind, and he rubbed his hands across his eyes. He had tried calling Lucy every day for a week without success. Oscar and Owen were crying every night, wanting their mother. She had been gone six months. Getting her on the phone had become harder and harder. That evening, when he had finally got the kids in bed with Sadie's help, under the light of the full moon, he'd walked down to the creek behind their house. He'd written his hurt down in a notebook, then pulled out his fiddle, adding the mourning notes to the words pouring from his soul as the haunting moon bathed him in a soft, lonely light. When his sorrow was spent, the anger took over. He slammed the fiddle against the rock where he sat, then threw the broken instrument that was so much a part of him into the water, murky from the recent rains.

"Dad?"

Orville pulled in a deep breath and looked at Olivia. "What did you say?"

"I asked you why you don't play anymore. You could have

been playing in the church band all these years or just playing with Ori, or even teaching me."

Orville looked from his daughter over to Lucy. Her eyes met his, a begging look of understanding filling her face. "It was a part of something that was over." Orville's words weren't hard, but finite, set in stone. "Something that wasn't coming back. I let go of the music when I let go of the hope of your mother ever returning."

Chapter Eight

Lucy pushed the microphone back and smiled at the dinner crowd, clapping for her last song. It had been a month since her first show at the Blue Hotel, and Gordon had been right, as usual. The people came to hear her, welcoming her, and her new style of singing into the Red Creek community as one of their own. She didn't need the big band and flashy show behind her to entertain the home folks. Her singing her songs, expressing her love of life and her newfound love for Christ were enough. She squeezed her eyes shut. *Thank you, Lord, for not casting me out, for pulling me to you even when I was running away.*

She opened her eyes and stood from the little stool. She scanned the crowd, looking for Gordon, knowing he would be in the back. He had been such a dear friend through the years. The money she'd scrimped and saved twenty-three years ago to buy a bus ticket to Nashville and live off of until she could find a job had been a fraction of what she'd needed. Orville hadn't gone to the bus station with her. He and the kids said their goodbyes in the front yard, and Sadie reluctantly drove her. Gordon, then married with a child of his own, was waiting on the bus for her, sitting on the front seat when she entered.

"Take this," he said, shoving an envelope in her hand. "And promise me you will send me your address when you get there and find a place to stay."

"How did you know I was leaving today?" Lucy had looked down at the thick envelope, then back to her friend, her and Orville's friend.

"Word gets around." Gordon didn't give any other explanation, squeezed her hand as he stood, giving her his seat. "Send me your address. Promise?"

"Gordon." Lucy opened the envelope and stared at the money inside. "You don't need to do this. Your wife and son may need this."

"My wife and son have everything they need. You still haven't promised."

Lucy swallowed. "Yeah. I'll send you my address."

He'd stepped off the bus without another word, and Lucy left Red Creek, fully intending to stay in touch, not only with Gordon, but Orville and her family. She also planned to keep all the promises. She would find someone to listen to her music, make a record, then somehow convince Orville to move their family to Nashville with her. Lucy's lips molded into a tiny smile at how naïve, how plain dumb she was back then.

She sent Gordon her address and called Orville when she arrived. That was the only part of her grand plan she'd honored. Instead of making a splash on the music scene, she'd made a splash on the kitchen scene, finding a job as a waitress to make ends meet. The tiny hole in the wall apartment took every dime of her money and an enormous chunk of the money Gordon had given her. After a couple of months of working her fingers to the bone at the restaurant during the day, and trying to figure out how to make connections in the music community in the evenings, the money was gone. She was ready to throw in the towel and go home where she belonged. At just that moment, she found in her mailbox a sealed envelope with nothing but money; no name, no explanation, just cash. Not a ton of money, but enough to keep her afloat for another month, another month to make a go of it and figure out how to make her dream come true.

She'd never contacted Gordon to thank him. Somehow, with them both being married, it hadn't seemed right. The envelope hadn't been mailed; it would just be in her box every month. Later, when she'd started gaining a little traction and could afford a better place, she'd left a note in her box telling whoever Gordon hired to drop off the money that she was moving and didn't need his help anymore.

It surprised her to find the money in her new mailbox at the end of the month again. It hadn't mattered after that. Over the years, as her music career grew, and she'd started touring, no matter how long she was gone, when she returned home, the envelopes, one at the end of every month, would be there. Had Gordon's wife resented him doing this for her? Had she found out and thought there was something between them and that's why she left? She'd put notes in the box several times, telling him she didn't need him to do this, but he never acknowledged them.

After all those years of silently supporting her, who was she supposed to call when the cancer took away all the glamour and glitz? The woman she thought she was had been taken away. Not Orville. She'd abandoned him and their family. The words hurt, but they were true. Seeing him that Sunday afternoon, the look of pain on his face when Olivia asked him why he'd given up his music, had driven home even harder what leaving had done to him. She knew he'd suffered, knew her leaving hurt him, but until then, she'd never truly realized the pain she'd caused him. What was he thinking that afternoon? What memory triggered when she handed him the guitar?

She swallowed down all the memories. Since that Sunday, she visited with the kids several times. She'd been to Olivia's restaurant often, helping her work and get ready for the upcoming grand opening. She was even planning on singing that night. She needed to talk to Gordon about that, too. He might not like the idea, but oh well. He knew she was here to reconcile with her family first. The music was no longer front and center in her life. The Blue Hotel would have to do without her for one night.

Several people stopped her as she weaved through the tables. She spoke to everyone, thanking them for listening, talking about the town, and relating how she was glad to be home. A few people asked her to sign something they brought with them, one of her CDs from over the years, or even sign an autograph book. A lot of the folks were locals, but more and more people were tourists, traveling through town for a stopover on their way to the beach.

She finally made it to the back of the restaurant. Gordon was nowhere in sight. Oh well. She'd talk to him about singing at Ollie's place another time. She stepped from the restaurant into the hotel lobby and pulled in a deep breath.

"You sound as good as ever." Orville stood just outside the restaurant in the lobby, dressed in his usual jeans and brown button-down work shirt. A little thrill ran through her stomach as she smiled up at his sky-blue eyes. Those eyes and that voice would always affect her. It wasn't anything she could help, and it didn't mean anything. He was just a good-looking man and always would be.

"Thank you." She licked her lips. "I'm trying to infuse a little of my faith into my music. Can you tell?"

"I can."

Her pulse quickened as he continued to stare down at her.

"Are you here to see Owen? I can help you find him if he hasn't already gone home for the day."

"No. I, uh." Orville rubbed the back of his neck with his large tan hand. "Actually, I came by to hear you sing. The kids keep nagging me to do it, so I figured I could drop in before they worry me slap to death."

"I'm glad you did." Lucy grinned. Same old Orville. "Well." She rubbed her hands together in front of her. "You want to go into the restaurant and grab a bite to eat? I don't eat until after I'm done singing, and I'm starved."

"Hmm." Orville looked over Lucy's head at the people sitting at the tables, most in clothes fit to wear to church, then down at his shirt and jeans. "No, I guess not."

"I have a better idea." Lucy's eyes sparkled. "I have an enormous ribeye thawing in the fridge. It's huge, and I usually make two meals out of one. Come up to my room with me, and we can eat there."

"Are you sure?" Orville's brow wrinkled. "I don't want to take the food from your mouth. I have leftovers at the house if the young-uns haven't eaten them already."

"Of course I'm sure." She grabbed his hand and tugged him toward the elevator. "It will be nice to have company for dinner." They stepped into the empty elevator, and Lucy looked down at his hand, calloused from years of working outside. Heat crept up her neck at the ancient memories of his hands and how they made her feel in days long gone.

She dated while in Nashville, justifying in her mind that she had divorced Orville with her heart, even if he hadn't signed the paperwork. She'd even had a few one-night stands. What had she ever seen in Cal Warren? How had she believed for all those years that she was saved? She was baptized at the age of eight after a week of vacation Bible school. Her friends were all repeating the sinner's prayer and walking the aisle, so she did it too. The truth, the hard truth,: however, was, if she'd died before last year when God had opened her eyes to the truly wretched creature she was without Him, she would have busted hell wide open.

She eased her hand from Orville's, glancing up at him. He stared at her, a strange expression on his face. "What do you think of my act?" She needed those elevator doors to open so she could put some distance between them without looking so... obvious. What was taking so long? Why was being around her soon to be ex-husband making her have butterflies?

"You've improved on the guitar." Orville continued to stare. He reached his hand toward a single crazy curl that had escaped the comb attempting to hold it in place. "How do you make your hair do this now?" His big fingers gently tucked the curl back down, but it sprang back up with a life of its own as soon as he moved his hand. "It's so different from your old hair."

"You don't like it?"

"I do." Orville nodded and narrowed his eyes, looking at the curl again. "It's just that when I close my eyes, I see the old you. It's still sort of a shock to see this." He dipped his head toward her curls.

Before she could answer, the elevator doors finally opened. Did he still think about her very often? Or was he making conversation? Who was she kidding? Orville Robinson never said anything to just make conversation. If he asked something, he really wanted to know. Polite talk was not a skill he had ever mastered.

She stepped into the hallway, and they walked the short distance to her hotel door. He stood behind her as she pulled her keycard from her purse. She could feel him, his closeness, and again, a ripple of something pleasant, but a little unnerving, ran through her. *I'm marrying Gordon. All of this, whatever this is, means nothing.* She hurried into the hotel room and dropped her purse on the small table in the entryway.

Space... she had to put some space between them. "Take a seat." She didn't look over her shoulder as she stepped into the kitchen area. She hurried to the refrigerator and opened the door, leaning into the cool air. She closed her eyes, attempting to pull up Gordon's face in her mind. This had not been a smart idea.

"What are you doing?"

Lucy jumped like a scared cat with a wolf on its heels. "Fixing dinner." She grabbed the steaks. "Go sit down. I've got this."

"I think I'll help."

Lord help me. This was not smart... not smart at all.

Chapter Nine

"When did you start helping in the kitchen?" Lucy turned to face Orville, keeping the cold platter of raw ribeye steak between them like a talisman, warding off some sort of powerful wizard.

"When did you learn how to cook?" Orville took the platter from Lucy's hand and stepped over to the bar. "This is a nice-looking cut of meat. Unless you've improved over the years, it's fixing to be burned beyond recognition." He looked around the little kitchen and turned to the stove. "Where do you keep your skillets?"

"For your information, the reason most of our meals were burned back then was because I was always distracted. Somebody always needed a bottle or a diaper change or help with homework or I was breaking up a fight or heaven knows what else." She walked to the stove and opened the oven door. "Here. I use this cast-iron skillet. Get it hot so it will sear the outside of the meat. I like mine about four minutes on both sides." Orville's hand brushed against hers as he lifted the skillet to the burner, and another thrill ran through her gut. She backed away and opened the freezer to grab a bag of frozen broccoli. "You never answered my question. When did you get so handy in the kitchen?"

"Can you keep a secret?" He pulled the damp plastic off of the platter of steak. "Where's the trash can?"

"Under there." Lucy pointed to the sink. "I can keep a secret." He still had a good head of hair, still wavy, just sprinkled with silver now. He looked good in silver.

"I can cook a steak, fry bacon, scramble an egg, and do a few other things in the kitchen. When I'm by myself at the house, and it's time to eat, I fry up a steak and open a can of pork and beans or corn or something."

"But you keep it a secret so everybody will wait on you hand and foot." Lucy chuckled and rolled her eyes. "Orville Robinson, that's not right and you know it."

"I'm not broadcasting it to the world, no." Orville opened the cabinet above the stove and took out the salt and pepper. "Just because I can grill a piece of meat and open a can doesn't mean I can cook for myself all the time. You know Sadie's a good cook, and Ollie is, too." He grinned as he shook the spices on the ribeye. "Why give up a good thing? Besides, I do a lot of things for them in return for the meals they cook for me."

"I know you do." Lucy stepped over to the counter, pulled out a pan, and started preparing the broccoli. "You've done a great job with our family, Orville." She plopped butter in the pan and waited for it to melt. "We have amazing children."

"Yes." Orville stepped beside her and put the ribeye in the hot skillet. The cold meat sizzled as it connected with the cast iron. "We do, but I have to tell you, Lucy. They've all been so happy to have you back."

"Except for Oscar." Lucy kept her eyes on the pan in front of her, pouring the broccoli over the melted butter, then covering it with a lid. "I'm not sure he will ever forgive me, and I can't blame him if he doesn't. Leaving you was terrible... but leaving my kids." She pulled in a ragged breath. "It's shameful." She reached up and stuck her hand in her curls, massaging her scalp. She looked up at Orville, his blue eyes staring down at her. "I can't undo it. Heaven knows I wish I could, but I'm not that woman anymore, you know? All of them, except Oscar, are starting to believe I've changed." She blinked, not allowing herself to look away. Refusing to let her past mistakes control her. "I hope one day that you'll believe me, too."

Fifteen minutes later, they were sitting at the little table near the sliding glass door that overlooked the forest behind the hotel. The steak, broccoli, and potato salad Lucy had picked up from the grocery when she got the meat earlier was slowly disappearing from their plates.

Orville hadn't planned on coming to the Blue Hotel tonight. True, he had driven by the hotel almost every evening when he closed the store. A few times he'd used the excuse of checking to make sure Sadie wasn't still out on the side of the road selling watermelons that close to dark. The idea that his sister would actually do that was utterly ridiculous, even in his own head. He'd then tell himself he was going out to Olivia's restaurant to see how the place was looking. He'd drive past his daughter's place and turn around at the hotel, so Olivia wouldn't know he was checking on her. Finally, he quit trying to fool himself. He wanted to find out if Lucy was drawing a sizable crowd to hear her sing. She was.

It was true that the kids had mentioned he needed to go see her show. It was also a fact that if he hadn't wanted to, no amount of nagging from his children could have gotten him there... yet there he was. Sitting across from his estranged wife, laughing as she told him about the time she accidentally pulled the toupee off of the host at a benefit concert.

"Lucy." He set his fork on his plate and leaned back in his chair.

"Hmm?" Lucy smiled across the table.

"You've changed." Orville squinted his eyes, trying to bring his thoughts into focus. "I mean, you look different with that crazy hair, but that's not what I'm talking about." He tilted his chin down, watching her face. "What happened? What really happened to you?"

Lucy sipped her tea, taking her time before setting it down. "Over a year ago, close to two, I went in for my mammogram. I had been putting it off all winter, but finally made it to the clinic to have it done."

Orville didn't say anything, didn't move. His eyes focused on Lucy. "Well." Lucy rubbed her lips together and looked away from Orville's intense gaze. "They found a lump in my breast. To make a long story short, I had a mastectomy, chemo, and radiation." Her hand raised to her chest, adjusting her shirt near her collarbone. "It was a hard time for me. I... realized how alone I had allowed myself to become." Her lips pulled into a nervous smile, and she finally looked away from Orville to the scenery below the glass door. "Fame doesn't seem that important when you are laying in a hospital bed wondering if you are going to live through another Christmas."

"No." Orville frowned. "I don't imagine it does. But you seem, I don't know. Good. Not like somebody who just got through fighting cancer."

"Oh, I am." Lucy sighed and turned her gray eyes back to Orville. "The hospital chaplain came by after one particularly rough day of puking my guts out. I was sitting on the side of my bed crying like a bald-headed baby. He sat beside me, handed me a wet washcloth, and asked me if talking about it would help. After I told him all the superficial stuff, like how the cancer had ruined my body and nobody wanted to see a middle-aged, bald-headed country music singer, he asked me if that was really what was bothering me." She shrugged her shoulders and looked down at her plate, picking up a tiny speck of broccoli with her fingers. "After a lot more talking, telling him how I left my family to pursue my dreams, how I'd started having some success, but I still felt... empty, like I was succeeding on the outside with all the glitz and glamour, but on the inside, I was a withering lump." She dropped the broccoli on the plate and looked up at Orville. "He started explaining about how sin clings to us and separates us from God. How what I was doing was the exact opposite of what Jesus did."

"But you went to church your entire life." Orville crossed his arms over his chest. "You're the one that got me going to church."

"I know. But I was going to visit with our neighbors and friends. You know how I love to be around people, and with the kids being so needy, going to church was the only time I got to socialize with people my own age. I was as lost as they come, Orville. And now... I'm not."

"You sure put on a good show." Orville raised his eyebrows. "Until you quit returning my calls, I never would have believed you would have left us like that. I couldn't believe you weren't coming back. I didn't want you to go, but I was sure you'd be back."

"I didn't plan to stay gone."

Orville watched Lucy's eyes dampen with new tears.

"Then why?" He paused, his voice getting thick with emotion. "Then why'd you do it? Was being with me... with us... that terrible?"

"No." The tears started to trickle down her face. "It wasn't about leaving you. It was about chasing my dream, my way, on my own. Me, me, me." She shook her head, regret spilling from her voice. "At first I would tell myself that all I needed was a few more weeks before I would get that big break and then I'd come home and get y'all and bring you back." She sniffed and rubbed the end of her nose. "Then I was embarrassed by my failures, and it was easier to not answer the phone, to shove Red Creek and everything it meant to me to the back of my mind."

She coughed, clearing her throat. "Jesus left his home because He loved me so much that He was willing to give up the best of the best to make a way for me to be with Him. I left my home because I loved me and put what I wanted ahead of everyone else. My selfishness made me so blind that I couldn't see what I was leaving."

Orville watched Lucy lift her napkin from her lap and dab her eyes. She meant the kids, of course, not him, but she'd changed. God had moved in at her lowest point and changed her. He should tell her he'd sign the divorce papers and get them to her as soon as possible, but the words wouldn't come. He stood, pushing his chair back from the table. "I didn't mean to upset you, but I'm glad you told me."

"No." She looked up at him through tear-filled eyes. "I cry every time I think about it."

"I'm... sorry."

"No, no." Lucy stood and stepped around the table toward him. "You don't understand. I don't cry because I'm sad. What I did to the kids and you was terrible, that's true, but that's not what makes me cry. I can't believe that..." she swallowed and rolled her lips in, biting down to stop a sob. "I can't believe that Christ loved me enough to forgive me and give me another chance. I'm cancer free. He gave me a chance to come home—to undo. No, I can never undo what I did."

Her brow pulled low. "To ask for forgiveness from the children." She reached her hand up and touched Orville's arm. "From you."

Orville reached down and wiped the tear from her cheek with his thumb. "I wasn't the easiest person to live with. Plus, I could have gone after…"

"No, Orville." Lucy's chin tilted up. "This is *me* asking you to forgive *me*." Her tongue crept out and ran over her lips. "Forgive me?"

Orville's thumb trailed down and rubbed along her bottom lip. "God's forgiven you. How can I not do the same thing?" A longing, the one he had been pushing down for over two decades, pushed forward. He leaned down, breathing in the scent of summer sun and citrus from her skin. What would it be like to kiss her after all these years? To hold her against him like he had held no other person.

"Orville." Lucy stepped back right before his lips brushed against hers, her breathing quick. "Orville. I'm engaged to Gordon. We can't do… this."

Chapter Ten

I t was simple. He had two choices. There was no use beating around the bush and pretending about it. He could either continue on alone by giving Lucy the divorce and watch her marry Gordon like she planned, or he could hold off on the divorce and start pursuing her himself. The urge to kiss her last night started an entire sleepless night of possibilities. That wall he'd constructed year after year that had kept him from going to Nashville and begging her to come home crumbled with her two simple words... forgive me.

She'd changed, truly changed. He could see it, and he could feel it. He could feel something else, too. When he touched her last night, at first on accident, but later when he'd reached out to her, she'd responded. She hadn't wanted to respond, but that inferno that had burned between them all those years ago, the one that he had beaten down, tried desperately to smother out, it had started to spark. The heat was there exactly like before, and it would grow—if he let it. But a fire like that. It was out-of-control back then, blinding him to her imperfections, to her needs and her want to be her own person. He didn't want that.

What did he want, really? The first time he'd laid eyes on her, all those years ago, she'd been laughing at Gordon Blue. Gordon had puffed his cheeks out and shoved a couple of straws up his nose, acting like a nut, trying too hard to make her laugh, and it was working. He'd watched her, kept his distance for several days, but looked for her around town and at the high school functions he'd left behind when he graduated a few years before. After stalking her for a couple of weeks, he couldn't stand it. He wanted to meet this new girl in town. Seeing her with her friends—with Gordon, who was always nearby—was no longer enough.

Now, he'd come full circle. No, he did not want to spend the rest of his days watching Gordon Blue do everything in his power to make her happy. He didn't want to win her over from Gordon like a conquest and expect her to fall at his feet for the rest of his days either. He'd loved her back then, no doubt, but had he loved her the way he should have? The entire whirlwind had been out of control, driven by passion. The only intentional thing he'd done during that time of their lives was find a way to make her his, get what he wanted.

What had she said last night? Me, me, me? She had run away to live her dream because he had pushed her into living his. Back then, he'd never talked to her about what she really wanted. When she said she was leaving, going to Nashville to become a singer, he'd never thought she'd make it. He felt certain she'd be home in a couple of weeks, begging him to forgive her for running away and leaving the best thing that ever happened to her.

He'd been every bit as selfish as her. He'd had child after child with her, watched her struggle to keep up and raise their family with almost no help from him. He'd refused to leave the store, letting them barely scrape by because he'd wanted to have his own business. He'd been blind. No, not blind. He'd refused to see, refused to look beyond his own wants, his own goals.

He didn't want that again. No smothering her with the passion that had brought Oscar along after six months of marriage, a little too early for decency, and then the rest of the crew dropping in like little bundles of screaming joy on a factory assembly line. Last night, hearing her strum her guitar, close out her show with "Be Thou My Vision," singing with her eyes closed, the verses flowing from some place deep within her, he'd seen the real Lucy Robinson. The wall keeping her out had started to crack.

I want to. What? What did he want from her? *I want to make her happy. I want to give her... happiness and love. Give her...me? Not make her mine, but make me hers?*

"Dad." Ori's voice boomed along with his fist against the other side of the door. "You coming out of the bathroom anytime soon?"

Orville splashed cold water on his freshly shaven face and looked at his reflection in the mirror. *You're too old for this. How are you going to...court...date?*

"Dad?"

"Keep your pants on." Orville grabbed the towel from the edge of the sink and wiped his face. Couldn't a man have a minute's peace in his own house? "I'm almost done." He needed help on how to—woo her? His lips pushed up in a disgusted frown. *Definitely too old. If I want her back, I better figure out how to do this.*

What had happened? She had, and always would, think Orville was attractive, because... well... he was. Yeah, she was not the spring chicken she once was, but she wasn't dead either. That's where the little zing was coming from when they were together. She understood that and could control it. Once he gave her the divorce papers and she married Gordon, she would stay away from Orville. The physical attraction would cool down with time.

That didn't explain the rest of it. When he'd touched her face, when he'd leaned down. He was going to kiss her, and... well... she'd wanted him to. If she'd closed her eyes, it would have happened. Goodness. It almost happened with her eyes wide open. Afterwards, he'd seemed as shaken by the whole thing as her.

Did I do anything to make him think I was asking for a kiss? No. She'd needed to explain why she was back, how she was different, why she was asking for a second chance. She was passionate about wanting to make amends. Had he read her passion, her longing for his forgiveness as something more? Heaven knows her body sure responded to him, even when her mind was trying to do the right thing.

Oh well. She'd made it through the moment without doing anything she regretted. Time to move on. She dabbed on her lip gloss and headed downstairs. She was meeting Gordon this morning to discuss where to have the wedding reception. Gordon thought the Blue Hotel would be the perfect spot, and it would do. After seeing Olivia's restaurant; however, Lucy was envisioning something different. Something just as lovely, but with a more personal, family-type feel. Olivia would have the place going full swing by then. By then... they still had to set a date. She couldn't do that until she got those papers from Orville. She'd have to see him again, at least one more time.

She ignored the little ripple of pleasure in her gut from the prospect of seeing him again. Good grief. She had to get this under control. *I'm marrying Gordon. He's the one who's kept food on my table over the years. He's a good friend and deserves my loyalty.*

Her phone buzzed, and she answered it as she slid behind the wheel of her truck. "Hello."

"Hey, Lucy."

The sound of Orville's voice sent a quiver up her spine, and she swallowed. "Good morning."

"Look. I need to talk to you about something." He coughed, clearing his throat. "It's kind of important. Do you think we could have dinner again tonight? After your show?"

"I don't think so." The memory of his thumb running along her mouth flashed through her mind, and her tongue eased out and wet her bottom lip. "Can you tell me now? Over the phone?"

"No." The phone was silent for a couple of seconds. "This needs to be in person. How about lunch? Or dinner tomorrow night?"

"Well." Lucy bit her lower lip. Maybe he'd signed the papers. Maybe last night had not affected him like it had affected her. Her hand went absently to the mastectomy scar under the prosthetic on her chest. She was not the woman he had once known, after all. The spiritual and emotional changes were for the good, but the physical ones were not that appealing. She sighed. "Why don't I just drop by the store this afternoon? I'm meeting with Gordon this morning to go over some wedding plans, but I can come by after lunch. Will that work?"

"I'll make it work. And Lucy."

"Yeah."

"I enjoyed last night."

"Uh. Me too."

Lucy hung up the phone and frowned. What did he mean

by that? Did he enjoy the show, the food, the conversation? The almost kiss? Her phone buzzed again as she backed out of the parking lot and headed toward town. "Hello."

"Lucy." Gordon's voice filled her ear. "I'm sorry I didn't make it to your show last night. I heard it was another packed house."

"I don't expect you to make all the shows, Gordon. You know that."

"I know, but I want to be there for you. At least until you get settled in. I'll be there tonight. I was thinking that after the show we can have food delivered to your room. Have an intimate dinner, just the two of us. You've been so busy with your kids lately that we've not had much alone time. I proposed after just a couple of hospital visits in Nashville, then promised to be there for you when you moved here. I'm going to do better."

"Why don't we plan on dinner at the restaurant after the show?" Lucy's lips twisted from side to side. She didn't mind having Gordon alone with her in her hotel room. He was a gentleman and knew her boundaries. She just... wasn't in the mood. "Um. That way, I won't have to worry about cleaning up the place before or after. We can get a table in the corner and be off to ourselves."

"Okay." Gordon's disappointment was obvious. "I guess that will have to do. Are we still meeting to talk about the wedding in a bit?"

"Of course. I'm grabbing a coffee and a donut and heading to your office. Do you want me to get you anything?"

"No. My doctor has me watching my weight, remember?"

"I'm sorry. I forgot. I won't eat a donut in front of you." Her stomach let out a small rumble as she pulled into the donut shop. She had plenty of time. She'd get her donut and coffee and eat there. "I'll see you in a bit."

She put the truck in park and reached down to grab her

purse from the floorboard. A thump sounded on the driver's window and she jumped. She raised back up and smiled as Ori's grinning face stared at her through the glass, with Oliver a step behind him. *Thank you, Lord, for my family*. Would she ever get used to running into her kids, people she loved that seemed to love her in return, bumping into her like it was an ordinary thing?

She climbed out of the truck cab and received a hug from both men. "Let me buy you two a cup of coffee and a donut."

"You don't have to buy it, Momma," Oliver said, holding the door open for her to walk into the little pastry shop. "I'll get it."

"Long as somebody gets it besides me." Ori looked up at the menu on the wall behind the counter. "I'm spending every dime paying for repairs at Les's place, and then I have to pay my fines."

"I hope you think twice before you decide to crack a head through a plate-glass window." Oliver glanced at his brother. "You know the saying, crime doesn't pay."

"I hope I will too." Ori grinned at his baby brother. "But we'll have to wait and see, won't we?" He looked down at Lucy. "Momma, what did you do to Daddy last night?"

Heat crept up Lucy's cheeks. "What do you mean? He came to my show, then we had a quick dinner."

"He was as grumpy as a cat with a knot in its tail this morning when he left the house. He told me he saw you, and I thought you two had a big fight or something."

"No." Lucy stared at the menu ahead, avoiding the intense gaze of both her sons. "No. Nothing like that."

Chapter Eleven

Lucy pulled her truck into the run-down parking lot of Orville's junk store, bumping across a rough patch of cracked pavement, and easing into a faded parking spot. A SUV pulled out, leaving her vehicle the only one in the lot besides Orville's old truck parked near the entrance. Poor Orville. How did he keep the old place afloat? Gordon said the town was definitely growing in tourism and breathing new life into Red Creek. He was pushing the town council to encourage more businesses to the small town by giving the place a facelift with ordinances that promoted a more welcoming appearance. Could Orville's junk store survive that? How was it surviving now? He had to be hanging on by a thread. Even if the place was the ugliest building on the street, she didn't want to see him close. He did love his business so.

She flipped down the visor and fluffed her curls. It was almost three. She had been running late all day, ever since the impromptu meet up with her sons. Gordon had rescheduled a meeting instead of putting off their plans to discuss the wedding, but he hadn't been exactly thrilled about it. It didn't matter. Spending time with two of her boys was worth a little of Gordon's grump any day.

She laughed so much at the donut shop. Time had gotten away from her, and she ended up staying for an hour. How did she have two sons who were so different? Levelheaded, voice of reason, Oliver, and nutty Orion were like oil and water. No, not really. They somehow complimented each other. Even though their opinions differed on so many things, each seemed to bring out the good in the other one, lending some sort of balance, more like peanut butter and jelly.

She'd finally made it to Gordon's office, but only after Oliver said he had to go so he wouldn't be late for the high school boys' basketball practice. He reminded Ori he had to be at the store as well, but Ori said he had a few more stops to make before his workday started. "Pops is already as grouchy as homemade sin. Me being late couldn't make it any worse."

"Yeah." Oliver picked up their empty coffee cups and pastry wrappers from the table as he stood. "But why poke the bear, Ori? You know he's having a bad day, so why make it worse?"

"Because I can, little brother." Ori grinned a mischievous grin. "Because I can."

Lucy smiled as the overhead bell of Orville's store jingled, happy she'd spent her morning making new memories with her kids. Her shoulder leaned into the cool glass of the front door to push it open, her eyes adjusting to the dim fluorescent lights high above her head. She breathed in the never changing smell of old, worn-out things. "Orville?" Music floated from the back, an old Alabama song they used to sing together... there's an old flame burning in your eyes. She hummed softly as she made her way to the back of the store to the counter, taking in the merchandise. This place would take a lot of work to make it eye-catching, but it could be done with a little elbow grease and some money.

"Hello, Lucy."

Orville stepped into the aisle out of a display of some sort of tractor and farm equipment parts. Her heart started racing as she breathed in his familiar spicy scent. He'd obviously surprised her. That's why her heart was thumping in her chest. That was all it was. Surprise.

"Hello." She smiled and studied his face right next to hers. He didn't look grumpy now. Whatever had been bothering him earlier must have worked itself out. "Did Ori tell you I bumped into him this morning? We had coffee and donuts together. I hope he wasn't too late for work."

"No later than usual." Orville pulled a peppermint from his pocket and unwrapped it. "I decided a long time ago that Ori lives on an entirely different timetable than the rest of us. I'm not even sure he knows how to tell time."

Lucy breathed in Orville's scent again. "It's a good thing you don't let it bother you."

"It used to, but I finally figured out he wasn't going to change, and I'm not even sure he can, so I quit letting it get under my skin. If I hadn't, he'd had driven me to drinking years ago."

The five o'clock shadow, black, sprinkled with silver, that she'd noticed on his jaw last night was gone. She'd always loved him a little scruffy, even if his whiskers scratched her face when they.... She cleared her throat and took a step backwards, bumping up against an antique coat rack that had seen better days. "You needed to see me? I'm assuming you have the divorce papers ready for me?"

"No." He reached his arm up across her shoulder and steadied the coat rack behind her. "But I do want to talk about that." His hand dropped down, and he tucked a curl behind her ear.

Lucy sucked in a deep breath. *You just got through fussing*

*with Gordon about having the wedding at Olivia's restaurant.
You just assured him you were done being a Robinson and ready
to be a Blue. Get a grip, Lucy.* She ducked under Orville's arm
and stepped several steps away. "Well, let's find a table or some
place we can sit down and hash out whatever is on your mind."
And put some distance between us. Her head turned and searched
the roomy store crammed full of everything under the sun. "Do
you still have the office in the back where the kids used to play?"

"I do." Orville stepped past her and her body, the treach-
erous louse, reacted again to his nearness. "Follow me."

Lucy walked down the aisle behind Orville. His shoulders
were still broad and straight, maybe not as muscular as they
were twenty years ago, but he was definitely in much better
physical condition than Gordon. Her eyes narrowed. *What
are you doing? What does it matter who was the best looking...*
she swallowed... *body?* She forced her eyes from the man in
front of her and looked at the store. "Do you do a lot of
business?"

"Enough." Orville stepped behind the display case in the
back that doubled as a counter and opened up a door over to
the side in a little alcove. "We can talk in here."

"What about customers?"

"If the bell rings, I'll hear it."

Lucy stepped past Orville and walked across the office of
sorts and sat down at an old wooden table. It wobbled a bit
when she set her purse on top.

Orville shut the door behind him and turned. He put his
hands on his hips as he stared at her. Yes, something was up.
He wasn't grouchy, but something was definitely on his mind.
"Take a seat, Orville, and tell me what's bothering you. Have I
done something with the kids you don't agree with? I know
you didn't like that I bailed Ori out of jail, but I thought we
had worked that out. Next time, and Lord willing, there won't

be a next time, but if there is, I'll call you before I do that. We can come up with a plan together."

"No." Orville's lips pushed into a thin line, and he stepped over to the table. "Lucy, last night when I got home, I figured something out."

He picked up an old chair from the other side of the table and set it right next to Lucy's. So much for keeping a little space between them. He sat down, so close that his knees brushed against hers. "Lucy." His eyes searched her face. "I thought I pushed you out of my heart years ago. I really did. I never looked for another woman to take your place because..." Consternation filled his eyes. "I knew you were, and always would be, the only woman in my life. I didn't want anyone else... and..." He set back in the chair and raked his hand across his face.

"Orville." Lucy's stomach tightened. "I enjoyed our dinner last night, but I'm engaged to Gordon."

"But you're not married to him yet." Orville put his hands on his knees. "Lucy, we belong together. Always have. We messed it up the first time, but we can..."

"Orville." Heat rushed up Lucy's neck. "Stop. I'm engaged to another man. Your best friend."

"He hasn't been my best friend since you picked me over him when you were a teenager." He shrugged his shoulders. "We get along fine, not that I care a hill of beans about that, anyway, but he's not my best friend." He leaned forward, his face inches from hers. "Lucy, you do something to me that no other person on the face of this earth does." He reached up, his hand cupped her cheek, his fingers stroked her skin. "And I do the same thing to you. You know it's true."

A burning, a deep hot longing that she hadn't felt in years suddenly tore at Lucy's middle, and she leaned forward. Her lips found Orville's and everything that had died in her, everything she had slaughtered so her dream could live, came rushing back. His hand moved from her cheek to her shoulders and pulled her to him. She didn't think, couldn't think. She allowed him to hold her close in his arms, to kiss her like he used to, like Gordon Blue or no other man ever had.

"Well, lookie here."

Lucy's eyes flew open, jerked from the passionate place she was heading, a trip she had no business taking, to the door where Ori stood. She pushed against Orville's chest. When? How had she gone from her chair to his lap? She jumped up, slapping Orville's arms away as he tried to keep her where she was. "Ori. This is not..."

"Oh yes, it is." Orville held onto her hand, standing with her as she attempted to pull away.

"No." Lucy scowled at Orville and jerked her hand from his. "It most certainly is not!" She tugged at her blouse, straightening it where it had twisted while they were.... Her cheeks blazed. What was she doing? What would Gordon say when he found out she was in the backroom of the junk store making out with Orville?

"I'm not the most educated Robinson in the clan on most subjects." Ori's eyes crinkled with amusement. "But I believe I'm pretty well versed on what is going on back here." He looked at Orville and chuckled. "Way to go, Pop."

"Hush, boy. That's your mother you're talking about. Don't make me whip your hide, because I can, and I will."

"Sorry, Pop. Momma, you know I don't mean any disrespect." Ori's eyes sparkled, not looking the least bit sorry about a single thing. He took a step backwards, easing the door closed in front of him. "I'll just let you two get back to it, then."

"Oh. No. You. Won't." Lucy snatched her purse from the table. The unsteady furniture wobbled and rumbled with the sudden movement, just as off kilter as she felt at this moment. "Ori Robinson, you stop right there. This is not. Well, this was not supposed to happen, and it will not be happening again." Ori opened the door and propped his shoulder against the door frame, clearly enjoying the show. Lucy felt the steam rising out of her ears. "Ori, wipe that smile off your face right now, young man, or I will let your father do what he said he was going to do."

Ori stood up straight and did a mock salute. "Yes, ma'am."

Lucy whirled around and glared at Orville, looking much too pleased with himself. "And you, Orville Robinson, I want those divorce papers signed, and I want them signed now."

"Not going to happen, Lucy." Orville smiled at Lucy, his hand steadying the table, his face calm, almost glowing.

"Oh, yes, it is, Orville Robinson." Lucy looked back at Ori. "And you. Don't go flapping your gums about this... to anyone. You hear me?"

"Loud and clear." He winked at his father. "Just so you know, I'm on your side in all this, Pop. I like Gordon and all, but I can't really imagine him as a Robinson."

"He's not going to be a Robinson." Lucy pulled her purse on her shoulder and walked over to Ori. "I'm going to be a Blue. You might as well get used to it, because it *is* going to happen." She pushed past her son and stomped out of the store. This day was not going as planned. Not at all.

Chapter Twelve

"So, what's the plan, Pop?" Ori listened to the bell jingle as his mother rushed from the store like a lion was on her heels. "Is that why your nose was so bent out of shape this morning? You were worried Momma would turn you down cold? Doesn't look like you have much to worry about from what I saw."

"You go ahead and forget what you saw." Orville picked the chair up and put it back where it belonged on the other side of the table. "This is none of your concern."

"I can let it slip to Owen that I saw you and Momma smooching, and you know Owen. Gordon Blue will know all about it before Owen can take a breath. He can't keep his mouth shut to save his life."

"You'll do no such thing." Orville walked past his son, still standing in the doorway, and looked around the store. "You promised your mother you'd keep this a secret." He turned and raised one eyebrow, staring at Ori. "If you know what's good for you, you'll keep that promise."

"Alright." Ori raised both hands in surrender. "I'm simply trying to help things along, but you do this your way." He grinned again. "You seem to be doing a pretty good job of..." He stopped as Orville's other eyebrow raised. "Okay. I'm done."

"About time." Orville looked under the counter and pulled out a piece of paper and an envelope. "Get the Gibson out of the window and take it out to this address. Clint Hudson is expecting you. He's buying that guitar, but I've done business with him in the past. Show him this letter where I had it appraised. He's going to offer a low bid, but..."

"Don't worry." Ori took the paper and the envelope. "If he can't come within fifty bucks of." He paused and opened the envelope, letting out a low whistle at the amount of money from the appraisal on the paper. "I guess you were right about that old six string."

"Surprise, surprise," Orville mumbled, his mind still on Lucy. "If he agrees to the price and shows you the money, then do the deal, otherwise, bring back the guitar."

"You know. If you cleaned that guitar up and put it on the webpage."

"Would you do as you're told?"

"Sure thing, Pop." Ori started toward the front of the store, used to Orville barking orders. "I'm just trying to keep this place afloat."

Orville ignored his son as his fingers ran across his lips. He'd been right. She was still as affected by his touch as he was by hers. That had to mean something. She couldn't kiss him like that and still love Gordon Blue. He clenched his jaw. She wasn't kissing Gordon Blue like that. Was she? She was engaged to the man.

The bell over the door jingled, and a couple of minutes later, Ori's truck disappeared from the parking lot. Orville hadn't planned to kiss her like that today. He had planned to explain to her how he wasn't the man she'd left all those years ago. He was going to ask her to give him a chance, a few dates to prove that they could rekindle what they had, and it would be better than anything she could ever have with Gordon Blue. That had been the plan, but when he'd touched her, she, well... she'd reacted like she'd always reacted in the past. And, of course, he'd reacted right back. A slow smile crept across his face as he thought about her jumping out of his lap, anger shooting from her eyes. Yeah, the day Gordon Blue could handle that woman would be the day it snowed in Alabama in August.

Lucy walked into the choir room the following Sunday and pulled one of the white satin robes from the rack. She needed to get into the spirit of worship, and singing hymns would help that along. The way she'd felt for the past couple of days was anything but Christian. First there was Orville doing this flip-flop on her, being all nice and sweet, and... smug. He knew. He knew good and well that she had a weakness for him, and the old fink was trying to take full advantage of it.

Then there was Gordon. The man who owned half the town and ran one of the largest businesses in the state was suddenly an insecure twelve-year-old boy. She told him she was marrying him. She was wearing his ring, had never given him any reason to doubt her sincerity, except for the one, well, almost two times with Orville. But that wasn't her fault. If Orville would just turn back into his grumpy old man self, and Gordon would man up, then she could get on with her life.

She took the song book one of the ladies handed her,

smiling and pretending to listen to whatever all the excitement seemed to be over, but not really caring. So, they had another new choir member. That was great, but right now, all she wanted to do was sing. She followed the line of sopranos out, ignoring all the commotion behind her. She stopped at her spot in the center of the front row and her eyes scanned the crowd of churchgoers. The Robinson rows were both full, except for Orville's spot. He wasn't sick. Or at least he certainly hadn't been last night when he came to watch her sing, sitting in the front row and staring through the entire set. Gordon had started out at the back, at their usual table, but when he saw her looking down front, of course, he'd moved to the front too. Geesh.

Her eyes roamed from one of her children to the next, all seeming exceptionally happy today, smiling and nodding in her direction. She smiled back. They were a good-looking bunch, even if they were her kids. Olivia stretched her neck and continued to nod. What in the world? Lucy's eyes narrowed, and she turned to look over her shoulder.

"Hello, Lucy."

"You?" Lucy hissed, and Orville smiled like he didn't have an ulterior motive for being in the choir. "What are you doing up here?" He tapped his finger to his lips, shushing her. She jerked back around.

"Are you okay Mrs. Robinson?" The choir director whispered to Lucy. "Your face is flushed."

"I'm a little warm." She pushed her lips into a smile and fanned her face with the hymnal. "I'll be fine in a second." She lowered the song book, turned to the doxology, and began to sing when the leader gave the cue. The rich sound of Orville's voice, the deep baritone that was only his, reverberated around her, mixing with her soprano. The anger that had been there a few seconds before melted away as the sound of their voices blended along with everyone else's to praise their heavenly

Father. Orville might have had other reasons for being in the choir, or maybe he didn't, but the way he sang, the way his voice proclaimed the praise to God, that was something special, something she could not find fault with.

The song ended, and she bowed her head in prayer. *Lord, help me. I guess I don't really love Gordon like — well, like I should. It's not that I don't love him, I do, but not like...* She left the words unfinished, her brow wrinkled in thought. *If I... I mean when I marry him, I will be a good wife. I truly will, Lord. He deserves a good wife. He did so much for me. Help me to do right by him.*

The choir went down shortly after that and she tried to focus on what the preacher was saying, but her mind kept wandering. She smiled at Gordon sitting beside her, his Bible open to the passage, listening intently to the sermon. Was it fair to marry Gordon if she didn't love him the way he loved her? It seemed like the noble thing to do when they were in Nashville. She would give him the rest of her life in return for all the help he'd given her over the past twenty-three years. Now, however, it didn't seem noble at all.

Her eyes kept straying to the Robinson pews in front of her and on the other side of the aisle. Orville seemed to be drinking the sermon in, not the least bit disturbed by her presence.

"Little children, let us not love with word or with tongue, but in deed and truth." The preacher's words penetrated her thoughts, and she looked up to where he was reading from the Bible. But wasn't sacrificing her what—her freedom—to marry Gordon, wasn't that loving in deed? *It's certainly not loving in truth.* The idea pierced her heart, and she bowed her head.

A few minutes later, they were standing, singing the invitation and filing out toward the back. What had the sermon been on? She didn't have a clue.

"Momma?"

Lucy stepped into the bright noonday sun reflecting off the white concrete and squinted, looking for her daughter. "Gordon." She took her Bible from his hands. "Go ahead and get us a table at the hotel restaurant. I'm going to talk to the kids. I'll be along in a minute."

She watched Gordon stroll across the parking lot in his charcoal gray suit, his gray hair combed perfectly. He was a handsome man in his own way. She was lucky... no, blessed that he'd asked her to marry him.

"Momma?" Olivia touched her mother on the arm and Lucy turned. "Did you talk Daddy into singing in the choir? We had no idea he could sing like that."

"No." The corners of Lucy's mouth turned down, but she recovered her smile before Olivia noticed. "I had no idea he was going to be up there. But what do you mean you didn't know your father could sing like that? He used to sing all the time. He was even in a local band for a while before we married."

"Really?" Olivia's eyebrows shot upward. "Daddy in a band? I can't imagine that. First, we find out he can play the guitar and the other instruments, and now he can sing too." Her face creased with a smile. "What else is he keeping from us? Does he have any other hidden talents?"

"Well, I promised I wouldn't tell, but I found out he can cook, too."

"Your kidding?" Olivia's eyes stretched wide. "That old coot."

Lucy looked past her daughter to the people leaving the church and walking to their cars. "Where is the old coot, anyway?"

"I don't know." Olivia's eyes scanned the parking lot. "He usually makes a beeline to his truck before anybody can stop him to talk, but there's his truck." She turned back to Lucy. "I bet the song leader has him pinned inside trying to make him a permanent choir member. Oh, there's Quinn." She lifted her arm and waved to her husband, stepping away from a group of men a few feet away. "I've got to go." She leaned over and kissed Lucy on the cheek. "Love you, Momma. You might not have had anything to do with Daddy singing in the choir directly, but I think you're being home is having a positive effect on him."

Lucy watched Olivia walk away. She turned and walked back into the church house, not really sure why she was going back in. The foyer was empty as the preacher followed the last couple outside. Her eyes adjusted to the dimmer light, and she stepped into the cool sanctuary. There, down front, on his knees at the altar, was her husband, head bowed in silence.

She sat her purse on the back pew and walked to where he was; her steps quiet on the thick carpet. He looked up as she approached. "I'm sorry." She bit her lower lip. "I didn't mean to intrude."

"You're not intruding. I've made it right with the Lord, now I need to make it right with you."

Chapter Thirteen

O rville stood, his knees popping from kneeling down to pray at the front of the church. He wasn't a big fan of frills and fancy, but today the thick carpet padding the church's floors was a blessing.

"Look, Orville. This morning I admit I felt like you were invading my..." Lucy rolled her eyes upward and pushed her lips out in a pout. "I guess, my personal space when I found you behind me in the choir loft. But I was wrong, and I admit it. You sounded amazing. I actually got goosebumps when you started singing. But even if you'd sounded like a squawking chicken, it wouldn't have mattered. This is your church, too. You've come here a lot more than me. I had no right to think you were up there... for me."

Orville's mouth turned up in a slow smile. He'd missed so many things about her, but her fire, her spunk—he'd probably missed that the most. "Have you got a second?" He reached out and took her hand and the soft touch of her skin rumbled his heart, not with a hot passion like he'd had for her the other day, but with a longing, a desire to be her... man. "Can we sit down and talk? No games or tricks. I need to get the record straight."

Lucy's pink tongue darted out and ran over her lips. "Okay."

They sat down side by side in the front row. Orville let go of her hand and gathered his thoughts. "You were right about this morning. I was invading your space." She started to speak, but he held up his hand. "Let me say my peace, then you can talk." She slowly nodded. "I knew sitting behind you in the choir would ruffle your feathers, and, well, I kind of enjoy seeing you with your feathers ruffled." His lips pushed up in a lopsided smile. "You're awful cute when you get a little hot under the collar."

Lucy pursed her lips and tilted her chin down, obviously not thinking much of his explanation so far.

"Like I said, that was my intention." Orville paused and looked around the church, his eyes roaming down the rows of stained-glass windows depicting scenes from the Bible. He stopped on the one closest to the front, the scene of Jesus on the cross. He stared at the scene for a couple of seconds, then turned to Lucy, who studied his face. "This is not the place for my plotting and scheming, trying to figure out ways to trick you into spending time with me. You came here to worship the Lord, and I came here to turn your attention on me."

"Orville."

"No." He reached over and took her hand again, looking down at her delicate fingers in his big, calloused hands. "It was wrong, but the Lord convicted me of it with that very first song. When I started singing "praise God from whom all blessings flow," the words pierced my heart and well." He chuckled softly. "No offense, but." He looked at her face, watching him tenderly. "All thoughts of you and what had originally brought me to the choir flew out the window." He looked back up, nodded to the scenes around them. "This is a place to focus on God. What I did, trying to drag your attention away from Him and onto me, that was wrong. And... well." He squeezed her hand. "I'm through playing games. I love you, Lucy. I don't think I ever stopped. I just need you to hear that."

"Orville, you shouldn't say things like this to me. I'm engaged to Gordon."

"Yes, I should." Orville's eyes held Lucy's gaze. "You need to know how I feel. It would be wrong for me to give you the divorce and let you marry Gordon without at least telling you I love you. We deserve a chance, but the only way to have that chance is to be honest with each other, not with me trying to trick you or refusing to divorce you."

"If." The single word faded from Lucy's lips, and she looked away. "If I didn't love... you... like you love me... would you want to know?"

Orville's heart squeezed. *No, you do love me.* "I would want to know." He eased his hand away and stuck a finger under Lucy's down-turned chin, forcing her to look into his face. "It would hurt, but I would want to know."

"I've got to go." Lucy stood. "Thank you for being honest." She hurried down the aisle, grabbed her purse and Bible, and continued out the church doors, not looking back.

Orville stood, suddenly feeling twenty years older than he had that morning. *She loves me. I can tell. I know. She has to.* He stared at the doors she had hurried through a minute before. If she didn't admit she loved him, if she went through with the divorce and married Gordon Blue, it wouldn't matter if he loved her or not. Yes, it would matter.

He started down the aisle. His steps slow, weighted down with the impact of her words, the impact of his love. He couldn't reel it back in, shove it back down where it had stayed while she was away, out of his life. No, he would always love her. Even when she married another man, he would still love her. How would he cope?

He stopped and looked back at the stained-glass windows one last time. *God, help me. You understand how it feels to love when it's not returned. Help me to... survive it.*

Orville was right. Lucy climbed in her truck and hurried from the nearly empty parking lot. She did not want to still be there when Orville came out. She needed to be alone, to think about what he said. If she didn't love Gordon, not the way she should, she should tell him. He had a right to know.

She drove through town on autopilot and pulled into the hotel parking lot. Would he kick her out of the hotel? Fire her from singing in his restaurant? Well, if he did, she would deal with it. She wasn't rich, but she wasn't a pauper. Having cancer had tapped into her nest egg, and there were very few gigs for an over the hill country music singer who was now very selective about the topic of her songs. Plus, she didn't want to leave Red Creek. She wanted to stay near... her kids. Orville's words rang through her heart. *I love you, Lucy. I never stopped. How can he love me? He doesn't even know me anymore.* She pushed the thoughts away. First, she would make things right with Gordon, even if it meant he never spoke to her again. Once this was done, she would decide what to think about Orville.

She made her way through the hotel lobby and into the restaurant. Several people stopped her, some were tourists who recognized her from her performances at the hotel, others were people from town that she was getting reacquainted with. She spoke with them all, not in any hurry to do what had to be done.

Gordon stood and held out her chair as she finally made it to the table. "I was beginning to think you had decided to eat lunch with your family and forgot to tell me."

"No." Lucy put a smile on her face. "I would never do that to you. Besides, when I spend time with the kids, you are more than welcome to come along."

"What held you up?" Gordon waited for her to sit, then sat back down in his chair. "I tried to call you, but I didn't get an answer."

"Hmm. I didn't hear it ring." Lucy's eyes narrowed. "I forgot. It's on silent. I always put it on silent before church." She took a sip of water the waiter set down in front of her. "I went back in the church for a few minutes to gather my thoughts."

"You seem a little flustered." Gordon's eyebrows drew together. "Lucy, is everything okay?"

"Actually, we need to talk." Lucy rubbed her hands together. Where to start? "Gordon, you've done so much for me."

"Nonsense, Lucy." Gordon reached across the table and took her hand. "Don't start that again. When I found out you were sick, of course I came to check on you. We've been friends since high school."

"There's that, but there's also everything else too." Lucy rubbed her forehead with her fingers. "The money."

"Lucy." Gordon released her hand, and she pulled it back. "I've told you before. The money was never missed. My wife or son never even knew I gave it to you, but like I said, you were a friend. I was helping you out."

"Gordon." Lucy pulled in a breath of air. *Here goes.* "Sending an old girlfriend money every month to keep her out of the poorhouse is more than most wives would understand. I don't blame them. We both know nothing ever happened between us, not before I left Red Creek. Once I got to Nashville, you never even came to see me until the cancer, but it does look a little, well, suspicious."

"Every month?" Gordon paused as the waiter returned. They gave their drink orders and waited for him to leave. "What money? What are you talking about?"

Lucy raised her eyebrows. "There's no need to be secretive about it now. We're engaged. Besides, nobody knows about it but me and you, but I want to talk about it."

"Lucy." Gordon stared. "I truly don't understand what you're talking about. I gave you five hundred dollars that day on the bus. That's it."

"No. I got money from you every month... an envelope in my mailbox every month, Gordon, come rain or shine." Lucy's eyes softened. "You don't know how grateful I am to you. For a while, that envelope every month was the only thing that kept me from living on the streets."

"That wasn't me."

"Gordon. It's okay, really."

"No, Lucy." Gordon frowned. "It really wasn't me. If I'd known you were in such dire straits, I'd have helped you, of course. When you didn't return to Red Creek, I assumed you were doing well. I didn't find out anything about what was going on with you unless I read about it in a magazine or newspaper, that is, until you called about the cancer."

Lucy flounced back in her chair. Gordon hadn't sent her the money? Then where had it come from? Not her kids. They were babies when the money started. Not Orville, he didn't have two cents to rub together. She'd asked her father years ago in a roundabout way if he was helping her out, and he had assured her that he was not supporting her wild haired lifestyle.

"Lucy? Did you hear me?"

"Hmm?" Lucy blinked. "I'm sorry. What did you say?"

"I said that since we're on the topic of money, I wanted to tell you that I'm going to rewrite my will and make you my primary beneficiary. My ex-wife is well taken care of, and I haven't made up my mind about what to do with Jonah. He'll be in prison a long time, so I have time to decide. That only leaves you."

A knot formed in Lucy's stomach. "Gordon. Can we talk about that later? My head is reeling. I've thought for the past two decades that you've been sending me money every month, a lot of money. Now I find out it wasn't from you, and I don't have a clue who was sending it."

"Oh, honey, I'm sorry. Of course."

"Where did that money come from?" Lucy's lips pushed together in a thin line. "Who's been watching me all these years? I changed addresses several times, and the money followed me."

"Whoever it was must not have meant you any harm." Gordon took a sip of his drink. "They gave you money. They must have wanted you to succeed."

"I guess." Lucy chewed on her bottom lip. "But it's still weird."

"It is. Have you gotten any more money since arriving in Red Creek?"

"No, I assumed that you stopped sending it since we were getting married."

"No." His eyes narrowed. "I can call a private eye friend I used when I got my divorce."

"No." Lucy shook her head. "I want to figure this out on my own." She did not need it to get in the papers that she had a stalker. She was nowhere near famous anymore, never had been much, but still, that kind of story always seemed to make it to the newspapers.

The waiter stepped up again to take their orders. "I'm glad we talked about that," Gordon said, looking over his menu. "It would have been too bad to have started our married life out on such a big misunderstanding."

Lucy raised the menu in front of her, not caring in the least what she had for lunch, but blocking her face from Gordon's view. "Who's wealthy enough to send me money every month for years? And how did they keep up with where I was?" She turned her head, taking in everyone around her. "And what do they want in return?"

Chapter Fourteen

A month later, Lucy pulled her truck into the crowded parking lot at the bank. Things were not going as planned, at least not in most of her life. Orville had practically disappeared. He sat behind her in the choir, but only said a polite hello. When she tried to talk to him about anything, his answers were short and stoic, definitely not like they had been before he told her he loved her. Other than that, she never saw him. She'd dropped by the store to question him about the divorce, but he was always in the back, too busy to talk. She'd even stopped by his house one Sunday after church at Olivia's urging. They waited and waited, but Orville never showed up for lunch. The kids, minus Oscar, tried to act like it was no big deal, but things had changed... yet again.

She couldn't blame Orville. He'd declared his love for her, and she'd walked away to be with another man, to break up with the other man, but Orville didn't know that. The break-up hadn't happened. After finding out Gordon hadn't been sending her the money, she'd been so confused, and even a little creeped out, that she'd dropped the subject. When she really got to thinking about it, she wasn't sure what to do. If she broke it off with Gordon now, he would know she was going to marry him because of the money, but would he think she was breaking it off because he wasn't her... sugar daddy? Bile rose in her stomach just thinking about it. She never considered herself a kept woman, but in reality, wasn't that all she had been all these years?

There was the other thing too, the thing that really bugged her. If she broke off her engagement with Gordon, would the money start again? She pulled her sunshades from her head down over her eyes as she slid out of the truck. An icy shiver ran down her spine as the end of summer heat blasted her in the face. Was she still being watched? She'd racked her brain for answers. There was only one other person who knew her well enough—long enough to have been sending her the money. She ducked her head and hurried toward the bank, weaving between the cars and trucks, bumping into a set of broad shoulders in her attempt to get inside. "I'm so sorry." She looked up at the man staring down at her, his eyes cool, his jaw set in a firm frown. "Hello, Oscar."

"Hello."

He tried to walk past, but she put her hand on his arm. She was making so much progress with all the kids, except him, her oldest. He was just as cold and unyielding toward her as he had been the day she'd first seen him. Would he ever forgive her for leaving? "Can we possibly get together and talk? I know you're angry at me, seem to hate me, even, but if we could just talk. If you would listen to me and let me answer any questions you have, you'd understand that I'm not the person I was when I left you and the rest of my family."

"Why?" Oscar stared down at her, his face unchanged. "Why do you care what I think about you? You're back. The others have accepted you in. Even Dad. That should be enough."

"Because, Oscar." Lucy winced from the pain in his words, the coldness in his voice. "You're my son, my oldest child. Until I can show you that I'm sorry, truly ask forgiveness and let you see who I am now...." She pushed her shades up on her forehead. "Until then, I can't have peace. I love you, son."

Oscar's jaw clenched tighter, but something flickered in his eyes. "Alright." He slipped his arm from her grasp. "I'll talk to you. Meet me tomorrow afternoon at my office. I get off at five."

Lucy smiled. "Thank you."

"I've got to go."

Lucy watched him walk away. She had to make him see that she had changed.

"It's my lucky day."

Lucy turned, pushing her shades back down over her eyes at the sound of the man's voice. "Cal? What in the world are you doing in Red Creek?"

"I'm here to see you, of course." Cal Warren, the only other person who could have sent Lucy the money, stood in front of her, smiling down with his usual charisma. The charisma that helped make him the star he was, the charisma that had drawn her in all those years ago. "I was on my way to the hotel to get a room. A little bird told me you are singing there." Cal wrapped his arms around Lucy and pulled her close, forcing his lips on hers.

"Cal." Lucy pushed him away, holding the man at arm's length. He chuckled, not the least put off, used to having women fall at his feet.

"I'm engaged to be married." Lucy looked over her shoulder through the rows of vehicles to Oscar's bright red pickup. Her son scowled at her through the windshield, his eyes as cold as ice. His truck hurried onto the street, tires squealing as he flew out of sight. She sighed and turned back to Cal. "You shouldn't have come."

"Honey, I almost let you get away before, and I've regretted it ever since." Cal reached up and lifted her hands from his chest. "I'm going to bring you back to Nashville with me or die trying."

"Go home, Cal." Lucy pulled her hands away. "What we had... it wasn't real." She walked past him and opened the bank door.

"I'm not going anywhere, Lucy," he said to her back. "You tell that rich boyfriend of yours that he has a little competition. I'll see you tonight."

Lucy walked up to the island in the center of the cavernous bank lobby and pulled a deposit slip from a cubbyhole. When she'd been diagnosed with cancer, when she'd needed a friend the most, she'd called Cal. He'd listened to her explain about the upcoming mastectomy, followed by radiation and chemo, how she'd lose her hair, how the chemo might affect her lungs, how she might never be able to sing again. He'd listened, assuring her he would help her get through it. Then he'd simply disappeared. She tried to reach him a few times, but soon it became obvious that Cal Warren wanted no part of the damaged Lucy Robinson she had become.

She tried making it on her own for several months, but the weakness, the loneliness eventually wore her down. That's when she'd turned to Gordon, thinking he was the one sending her the money all those years. Surely it was time to get together. If she didn't have long to live, and that's what she had been afraid of, it was time to let him know how grateful she was for everything he'd done.

She stared down, the deposit slip in one hand and the ink pen in the other. How had she gotten into this complicated mess? Did Cal really think he could waltz back into her life now that her health crisis was over? Apparently so. She scribbled down her account number for her withdrawal and walked over to the window. There were too many men in her life, too many complications.

It was time to come clean with Gordon, set Cal straight, and make peace with Orville. After that, well after that, she was done. She didn't care if she had to sleep in her truck and live on Vienna sausage and crackers. She was not going to be in anyone's debt, not going to pretend to be someone she wasn't. She had changed. *Lord, you know I'm not that person anymore. Why can't they all just see me, the new me?*

Because the new you is still pulling your old tricks, and you know it. Lucy climbed behind the steering wheel of her truck and slammed the door. Why did the voice of reason have to be so honest? Yes, she needed to tell Gordon she didn't love him. That was true, but that was it. *You have feelings for Orville.* Ugh. Sometimes she truly hated her voice of reason. Of course, she had feelings for Orville. He was the father of her children. *But you still seek him out like a bloodhound and light up like a Christmas tree every time he touches you.*

True. Although there hadn't been any more touching, and very little seeing lately. Okay. Come clean with Gordon, set Cal straight, and come clean with Orville. She swallowed, a slight tingle curling in her middle. What would Orville say about her taking money from whoever she had been taking it from? About her convoluted reason for marrying Gordon? What if the money had come from Cal? Who else could it have come from? What would Orville think about her relationship with the country music star? It would hurt him.

She eased onto the street and started toward the hotel. Her mind whirled with the task in front of her. She would not commit herself to someone she did not love. Not Gordon Blue, and especially not Cal Warren. He had always been fun, ready for a good time, but when things got tough, he'd disappeared. Plus, his belief in God was passive, to say the least. Exactly like hers had been when they met.

Telling Gordon her true motive for saying yes to his proposal would be painful because he was truly a sweet, good man. Running Cal off, that would be hard, but only because he was too pig-headed and too conceited to take no for an answer. Oh well, she could be pig-headed too.

She drove past Sadie Robinson, sitting beside Orville's old truck parked on the side of the road, the tailgate down, selling produce from the Robinson's garden. Sadie was another person she needed to make peace with. The list seemed to be getting longer and longer, but she would do it. She had to. And if she found another envelope full of money anywhere, ever again, she would write a note telling the sender that she could not, would not be bought.

That was not Gordon Blue kissing his wife. The man looked vaguely familiar. Orville sat in Sadie's truck, parked several vehicles away from where Lucy stood in the arms of a tall man dressed from head to toe in black, complete with a black Stetson. He'd watched her get out of her truck as he drove up. Watched her talk to Oscar, then watch her kiss this stranger right in front of the bank for anybody and everybody to see. What was she up to? He waited for her to walk into the bank, then he leaned over and pulled out the envelope holding their divorce papers, signed and ready to hand over to her.

He'd declared his love for her at the church. She'd said in a roundabout way that she didn't love him, but he hadn't believed it. He'd left her alone, given her plenty of time to see how much she missed him. He'd been sure she would come around. Hadn't she been seeking him out, coming to his store and to his house? Was she really only trying to get him to sign the divorce papers, after all?

A few minutes later, Lucy reappeared out of the bank. He ducked his head as she glanced around the lot and hurried to her truck. He watched her drive away, but still didn't get out of the vehicle. He'd said he wasn't going to play any more games with her, but here he was, still holding onto the divorce papers, playing hide and seek like a five-year-old. If she didn't love him, he couldn't make her, any more than he could make himself stop loving her. He put the envelope back in the glove compartment and opened the truck door. Tonight, after she was done singing, he would give her the divorce papers. She could marry Gordon, this other guy, or whoever else in Red Creek she was seeing. He couldn't stop her now, just like he couldn't stop her all those years ago. Lucy Robinson would do what she wanted to. Always had, always would.

Chapter Fifteen

Lucy ducked her head and hurried through the hotel lobby to the elevator. Cal's back was to her as he had a selfie made with many of his adoring fans. Was she like that? An attention starved puppy, not happy unless someone was making over her, propping up her ego? Possibly she was at one time but not now. She pushed the button and headed up to her room.

Cal had been a very big deal for a while. He was gathering a following, making a splash when they first met the night he came into the restaurant, and started hitting on her the second his behind hit the chair. She hadn't known who he was, but he assured her he was going places, and he had. Two years later, he had the biggest hit in the country. Eventually the song won a Grammy. He'd been music royalty and rode the wave of that song for about a decade, but he never had another hit as big as "Head Strong Love."

The elevator door opened on Lucy's floor and she stepped out.

"Momma." Owen smiled his usual excited smile at Lucy. "You will never guess who just checked into the hotel."

"Hmmm." Lucy reached her arm around her son's back and snuggled into a much needed, non-judging hug. "Cal Warren?"

"I should have known you would know already." Owen's footsteps fell in line with hers as they walked the short distance to her hotel door. "He said he's staying a couple of days, and Momma." Excitement radiated from Owen's face. "He said he would perform tonight. Here. At the Blue."

Lucy stuck her keycard over the door lock and grinned. She should take him to Nashville one day, introducing him to some of his favorite singers. "Of course, you turned him down, right?" Lucy looked up at Owen, forcing her eyes to look serious. "I can't let some washed up over the hill has-been have my stage."

"Well... uh... no." Owen's eyes searched her face. "I sort of told him he could do it." Owen stared down at Lucy. "I figured you would enjoy a night off." His lips twisted into a frown. "I guess I can go tell him never mind... if that's the way you feel."

Lucy's lips twitched at the torn look on Owen's face. How could he be so trusting, and Oscar be so suspicious? "No, son. I'm only kidding. Of course, Cal can perform tonight. Did you know that I opened for him back in the day? I even sang back-up on a few of his songs before I was singing on my own."

"I had no idea." Owen's grin reappeared. "One day I want you to sit down, just me and you, and tell me all about your Nashville life."

Lucy reached up and patted her son's cheek. "That would be nice." She stepped into her hotel room. "You want to come in? I can fix us some coffee."

"No, ma'am." Owen held open the door but didn't step inside. "I've got to get back downstairs and make sure everything is a go for tonight. When word gets out Cal Warren is singing here, this place is going to be packed. I better stop by his room and see if he is going to play his guitar or what he's going to do."

"Actually, I think he's down in the lobby signing autographs." Lucy bit her lower lip as an idea hit her. "Owen, Cal plays a little, but not really enough to perform without a band. Tell him I'll play for him, and I can get another guy as well. Knowing Cal, he's assuming you have a house band and hasn't considered that he might need to play for himself. If he has accompaniment already, don't worry about mentioning what I said."

"You're the best, Momma." Owen leaned through the door and kissed Lucy on the top of the head. "I bet you hear that all the time."

Tenderness filled Lucy's eyes, and she looked up at her son. "Not from the people who matter most. Thank you."

What in blue blazes was going on? Orville pulled into the grass along the shoulder of the road running in front of the Blue Hotel. Every park in front, behind, and along the sides of the hotel was full, plus, there were people in orange deer hunting vests directing traffic to park along the road and not take up the driving spaces that would block in the people in the parking spots.

He killed the truck engine and rubbed his hand across his jaw. He looked over at the glove box where the signed divorce papers waited. No, he'd leave those there. Why was this place so packed? Had something happened to Lucy? If there was some kind of Shriner's meeting going on, and all these vehicles had nothing to do with her, he'd come back and get the papers. Tonight it would happen. He'd slip the divorce papers to her tonight after the show. Wish her well in her new life with Gordon, then wait for that to implode. When it did, maybe she'd be ready to come home... where she belonged.

"Orville." Sheriff JT stepped beside him as he walked between the cars and trucks in the end of summer twilight. Fall was just around the corner, but the Alabama heat wasn't giving up without a fight. "I've been waiting for you to show up. Did you know Ori could play like that? It sounds like you used to play back when we were young."

"Ori?" Orville glanced over at his long-time friend, puffing and red-faced in the summer heat. Had Ori drawn this kind of crowd? No. Something else was going on. "What're you talking about, JT?"

"You don't know." JT shook his head and chuckled. "Figures." He reached up and grabbed Orville's elbow. "Slow down a second, and I'll tell you about it while I catch my second wind."

Orville stopped and turned, looking down at the pudgy sheriff. "I've got something I need to get done." He tilted his chin in the direction of the crowd of vehicles. "What's going on around here? What are you blabbering about Ori and playing?"

"Cal Warren is singing here tonight. You know who that is, don't you?" Sheriff JT stared at Orville. "He had that big hit several years back, 'Head Strong Love'..."

"Yeah, yeah, yeah." Orville frowned. "I remember the song. That explains the crowd." *And who Lucy was kissing on.* "What's that got to do with Ori?"

"Cal Warren is singing, but your wife and son are playing." Sheriff JT's face split into a grin, and he spat a puddle of tobacco juice behind him. "Orville, Ori is practically stealing the show. That boy can play and sing every bit as good as you can... or could." He wiped his arm on his sleeve. "Looks like you're as surprised about that as everybody else around here."

"I knew he could play—alright." Orville's eyes narrowed, remembering all the times Ori would suddenly stop playing the guitar in the store or at the house whenever Orville walked into the room. The boy had talent, had taken to the instrument like water to a duck when he was a kid. Orville should have paid more attention. Ori asked him to listen to him play when he was young, but Orville always found a reason to walk away from the music. From his son. Ori eventually quit asking.

"He can do a tad better than alright." Sheriff JT pulled his hat from his head and wiped his palm across his thinning hair. "I wonder if that's why he keeps going to Les's bar? I bet he's playing there."

Orville glared at the sheriff, then started back across the parking lot. "A bar is the last place he needs to be." Good, JT wasn't following him. He was tired of talking. and that man needed a two-by-four to the jaw to shut him up. He pulled open the lobby door, taking in the people standing around in groups. An electric guitar and an amplified acoustic played the introduction to a song he'd heard on the radio a few times. Sure enough, Cal Warren's familiar voice, the voice that annoyed him to the tips of his toes, filled the lobby. Applause exploded from across the room in the adjoining restaurant, and the people around him started clapping too.

"Excuse me." Orville tapped a man on the shoulder, someone he'd never laid eyes on, probably one of the many tourists that invaded their town for the summer. "Do you know who's playing for that guy?"

The man, wearing khaki shorts, a baby blue polo, and loafers without socks, looked at Orville. "That's Lucy Robinson and her son, Orion. I've never heard of him before, but he sang a song a few minutes ago while Cal took a break. Mister, that boy is going places." He turned back toward the restaurant door where the music continued. Orville's eyes scanned the enormous room as the song played through.

The song finished, and Cal Warren's voice filled the lobby. "Thank you. Now, I'd like to play a song that I'm sure all of you want to hear. This young man assured me he can play it and do it justice." Music Orville knew better than the back of his own hand began. A melody started that had nearly driven him crazy years ago before he'd finally shoved his longing, his anguish, into the prison inside of him. The room exploded with applause and cheers as Orville turned and strode from the lobby.

He swatted at a mosquito, weaving through the vehicles on his way back to his truck, the music growing fainter behind him. Thank the Lord JT was busy making an SUV back out of the fire lane. He crossed the road and climbed into his truck. What now? He pulled onto the road and flipped on his lights; the night creeping in on him like the memories he desperately wanted to avoid.

He'd talk to Ori, reason with him. Remind him that music was what stole his mother away all those years ago. Remind him that hanging out in the bar had landed him in jail—three times. He pulled on the truck's ancient steering wheel and turned around, heading toward home. It wouldn't do any good. He could talk until he was blue in the face, but if Ori had the bug to perform, the same bug that had bitten him when he was a teen, the bug that got ahold of Lucy, Ori would be gone.

He'd always told himself that the reason he'd stayed in Red Creek was because he hated change, hated the idea of living somewhere that wasn't home, but was that why? Truly why? He pulled into the long driveway leading to his house, the only place he'd ever lived. His truck dodged the biggest holes, but he still bounced along the gravel, unable to miss all the small bumps. He would get Ori to order a load of gravel tomorrow to fill in the washed-out areas.

Ori. Would he even be around tomorrow? Or would he be hitting the road with Cal Warren? What was Lucy thinking? Why had she brought that man here? Orville climbed out of his truck and started toward the porch but stopped. He walked around the house and through the backyard. The moon wasn't full tonight, but the sky was clear. There was enough light to find the path. He walked along, listening to the tree frogs calling for rain. An occasional lightning bug flitted across through the woods that brushed on either side of him. The soft soothing sound of water running along gently over rocks caught his ear as the path cleared, ending at an open area near the bank of Red Creek.

Orville walked over and perched on the cool rock where he had sat as a kid to fish. This was the same rock he sat on with Lucy the first time he had brought her here, the place he'd kissed her for the first time. The place they'd come again and again until he was once more, coming here alone. Why hadn't he packed up the kids and gone with her to Nashville? Was it for the kids? For their stability? He could lie to himself like he had been doing, like he'd allowed everyone to believe all these years. No, he picked up a rock and tossed it into the rippling water in front of him. The rock plopped into the water and sunk to the bottom.

No, time to be honest. He'd stayed because he was scared. What if he hadn't been good enough? What if he was just another man with a guitar and a longing to sing and that was all? Lucy had been brave enough to give it a shot, but he hadn't. He could have gone with her or even gone after her. He could have found a job, taken care of the kids in Nashville, and been with her... if he hadn't been scared. Now, here he was, alone and scared again.

"Daddy!" Olivia's voice floated down the wooded path leading from behind the Robinson house to Red Creek.

"Yeah." Orville got off his knees from his prayers and started back up the path, moonlight making the shadows dance around him. "I'm coming." He'd been sitting on the creek bank for two hours thinking and praying. Seeing Lucy kiss another man hurt, hearing Ori singing with Cal Warren, of all people, hurt. It was his fault, all of it. If he hadn't been a coward all those years ago, if he'd gone with his wife, if he'd at least chased after her when she didn't come home, she would still be his. Ori would not be singing with Cal Warren.

"I tried calling, and you didn't answer. Annie Jo said she saw you leaving the Blue Hotel in a hurry a while ago. I just wanted to make sure you were okay."

"I'm fine." Orville stepped up beside his only daughter. and they turned around, heading back to the house.

"You don't look fine." Olivia reached up and laid a hand on Orville's arm. "Are you and Momma not getting along? That man she used to sing with is in town. Is that what you're upset about?"

"I'm not upset." Orville listened to a whip-poor-will calling from somewhere in the woods. Another one answered a couple of seconds later. "I just needed some time to myself. Sometimes the creek bank is the only quiet place I can find."

"Dad." Olivia stepped in front of her father as the narrow path opened up by the big oak tree in the edge of their back yard. "Momma loves you. You and Momma are meant to be together. You need to talk to her."

"And you need to mind your own business." Orville stared down at Olivia's straight blond hair, glowing like a halo in the moonlight. "Your mother and I will work out our own affairs."

"Don't you think you should go talk to her?"

"I think I should go to bed." Orville stepped around Olivia and walked through his yard to his house. He opened the back door and looked back at his daughter. "Don't you have enough on your plate to keep you busy?"

"I'll always have time for you, Daddy."

Chapter Sixteen

Lucy took a bite of the cream filled doughnut and looked at the screen of her cell phone. Where was Cal? He said he'd meet her here at one o'clock. It was fifteen minutes past, but this was Cal she was talking about, so she probably had ten more minutes to wait. Last night had blown her away. Not Cal, of course. He was his usual self. He had a good voice, but not amazing. What Cal Warren had was stage presence, charisma. It didn't matter how good a person could sing. If they didn't connect with their audience, the show wouldn't be memorable. Cal connected, and so did Ori.

She had heard her son strum his guitar, knew he could play, but what he did last night amazed her, and everyone in Red Creek, as well. The kid played every bit as good as his father, and when he sang! If she closed her eyes, she would have thought it was Orville all over again.

She took a sip of her coffee, hiding her smile in her cup. God had such a sense of humor. The son that looked the most like her had the voice and the talent of his father. He had his father's abilities, but he obviously loved the singing, making music, and the stage like she did. She had thought years ago that Orville loved it too, but he hadn't. At least not the performing part.

"Hey, beautiful."

Lucy looked up from her coffee cup. "You're late."

"Am I?" Cal pulled the chair out from across the table and sat down. "Lucy Robinson, you've been holding out. That boy of yours is gonna be a star. Can any of your other young'uns do that?"

Right to the point. Cal always was a much better talker than listener. "I was as surprised as you about Ori." She set down her coffee cup. "I don't think my other children can play like that, but I'm not sure. Olivia says she plays the mandolin a little, but that's what Ori said about the guitar." Her eyes crinkled with a smile. "Wasn't he great?"

"The boy almost stole my show." Cal chuckled. "When I heard him singing during my break, I gulped down my coffee. If I'd left him up there too long, everybody would have forgotten who the star was."

"Maybe so." Lucy smiled politely. "Cal, I need to talk to you about something."

"Alright, honey, but first let's talk about your boy. I want to take him back to Nashville and introduce him to the right people."

"Hitching your wagon to a future star?"

"Aww, honey. I don't have to do that, and you know it. I'm just being a good friend to the boy's momma."

"Uh-huh. And maybe cut a single or two with Ori along the way?"

"That's a good idea, now that you mention it." Cal nodded, like the thought was new to him. "So, why don't the three of us sit down and talk? If you tell him it's a good idea, we could be on the road tonight, tomorrow at the latest."

"We can talk, but Cal, I need to talk to you about something else first."

"I'm all ears, beautiful. What's on your mind?"

"Cal." Lucy pulled in a deep breath. "Back when I first moved to Nashville, someone started—helping me, making sure I was able to stay in town to keep trying to make a go of things."

"Like I did when we first met." Cal reached over and patted Lucy's hand. "Those were some good days, weren't they, Lucy? You sure you want to stay in this little town and marry that rich boy? We could rekindle that old flame if you would come back with me and your kid."

"Listen to me, Cal." Lucy rolled her eyes. "This is important. Were you the one?" She stared at Cal's face. "Was it you who's been giving me money all these years?"

"Now, Lucy." Cal's eyes cut down to her hands, then back to her face. "You know I can't tell you that. Some things are not supposed to be talked about."

"Cal." Lucy's eyes narrowed. Was he acknowledging that he was the one? Was he trying to take credit for something without actually lying about it? Either one could be true with Cal. "Did you send me money every month? I need to find out who did it. I thought it was Gordon, but he says it wasn't him."

Cal flopped back in the chair. "Lucy, remember what I told you years ago when you showed me that money? Don't look a gift horse in the mouth." He scrubbed his hand over his face and looked up at the ceiling. "Can't you let it all alone? You have your health back, you have your voice back, you look fantastic, and you have a son who is going to take Nashville by a storm."

"Cal." Lucy raised her voice, then glanced around the nearly empty doughnut shop. Thank goodness they hadn't met during the morning rush. "Just tell me the truth," she hissed, leaning forward. "Tell me the truth or we're done."

"Yes." Cal leaned forward and squeezed her hand. "Okay? Are you happy?"

"Really?"

"Yes, Lucy. Yes, my secret's out. Now. Can we talk about Ori? About us?"

Lucy leaned back in her chair, studying the man across from her. "First of all, there is no us. When I needed you the most, as my friend, you bailed on me."

"Lucy, I'm sorry. I truly am, but I can't do hospitals."

"Whatever, Cal."

"What about your boy? Don't throw his chances of making it big down the drain because me and you are over. You know I can give him a leg up, just like I did you."

He was right. Cal had opened doors for her back then. Even later on, when she was starting to make a name for herself, opening for Cal had helped her career. He was a conceited, attention seeking oaf, but he obviously had a good heart, especially when he could profit by lending a hand. "I will talk to Ori today and call you tonight."

Cal slapped his palm against the table. "That's my girl." He stood up. "You're being smart, Lucy, but you can be even smarter. Give Rich Boy the boot and come on back with us. Even if we are over, your place is in Nashville, not here."

"No." Lucy looked up at Cal. "It used to be, but I'm not that person anymore."

Lucy looked across the couch at Ori. "Are you sure you

want to do this? It's not a decision to be made lightly." When she stepped off the elevator of the hotel after meeting with Cal, Ori was waiting outside her door, about to bust with excitement. He'd talked and talked about the performance last night and how much he'd enjoyed it, how he felt so alive on the stage.

She was right. Playing in front of a crowd brought him to life the same as it did her. She listened and laughed at his joy, then talked about Cal, and their conversation at the doughnut shop.

"Momma, are you kidding? This is the opportunity of a lifetime." Ori bounced up like a rubber band, completely different from the slacker, never serious about anything man he always pretended to be. "Making music, singing, this is all I've ever wanted to do. This is a dream come true."

"Son, it's not easy, not even with Cal's help. And you have to keep your head on straight. There are a lot of temptations..."

"Momma. I know. Believe me. Pop has preached the evils of alcohol, drugs, and loose living to me every day of my life." He sat back down. "I can handle it. You can keep tabs on me, whatever you want, but I need to do this."

"Alright." Lucy reached over and laid her hand on Ori's arm. "I'll set up a meeting with Cal." She looked at her son's glowing face. "You have a lot of talent, Ori. Way more than me or Cal. Make sure you use it in a way that pleases God, son. Your father is right. All those things are out there. Be careful who you attach yourself to. Cal is alright, but use your head."

"I will, Momma." Ori wrapped his arms around Lucy and pulled her into a tight hug. "I'm so glad you came back. I'm leaving, but not like you did. I'm going to keep in touch, come back around, bring you and whoever wants to come to Nashville to see me."

Tears spilled from Lucy's eyes. "Good. That's how it should be done. Don't give up one for the other." She pushed back and looked at Ori. "I love you and our family. I was selfish to leave all of you and stay away for all those years. I thank God He changed me, and I thank Him I get a second chance with all of you."

"How are things with Oscar?"

Lucy's eyes stretched wide. Ori was more perceptive than he let on. She wiped a tear from her cheek. "I've got to leave in a minute and go see him. I honestly don't know if he will ever forgive me for leaving y'all."

"If he doesn't, then he is the one who will suffer."

"But I will too. It hurts knowing he can't see the new me, how I've changed."

"What about Pop? He seemed to be coming around." Ori grinned and raised one eyebrow. "At least it seemed that way when I walked in on you two at the store."

"I hurt your father. He doesn't think I should marry Gordon... and he's right. Don't tell anyone, but I'm going to break it off with him, probably tonight."

"Good. That man could never be a Robinson."

"I was going to be a Blue." Lucy shrugged one shoulder. "But your father was... is right. You don't marry someone you don't love. It's not fair to that person. They deserve better."

"Mother of mine. You are a brilliant singer, a better momma, and I'm sure you are at the top of a lot of other lists, but there's one thing you could never be, and that's a Blue. You're a Robinson, always have been, always will be. I don't know why you're fighting it."

"You know what?" Lucy poked her lips out in a frown. "You need to mind your own business." She glanced across the room to the clock on the stove. "And I've got to hurry. The last thing I need to do is be late for my appointment with Oscar."

"You want me to tag along?" Ori stood from the couch. "If he starts misbehaving, I'll punch his lights out. Of course, somebody else will have to hold him while I do it, but I bet I can get Owen in on this action."

Lucy laughed. "No, I don't think that will be necessary, but thank you for the offer." She stood and tousled her son's soft blond hair, so unlike the brother she was going to see. "After I see Oscar, I'll talk to Cal and lay down a few ground rules."

"Ground rules? Momma, I'm not going off to kindergarten. Besides, Cal seems like my kind of guy. I'm sure we'll get along fine."

"You will." Lucy stepped over to the bar and grabbed her purse. "As long as things are going smoothly, and Cal thinks he's making a buck off of you, things will go fabulous."

"He doesn't strike me as a swindler."

"No." Lucy turned and ran her pointer finger along her bottom lips. "He's not. The thing is, Cal is always going to put Cal first. I don't think he knows how to be any other way. He will treat you right, help you meet the right people, but he will expect something in return." She put her purse on her shoulder and stepped toward the door. Ori followed. "I don't want him riding your coat tails once you are big—holding you back."

Ori stepped into the hallway and waited while his mother checked to make sure the door locked behind them. "You act like I'm going to hit it big. Is that my momma talking or Lucy Robinson, the country music singer talking?"

"A little of both, probably."

Chapter Seventeen

Lucy sat across the desk and looked out the picture window onto the street. A few cars moved along from time to time, but overall the scene was quiet. She leaned forward and strained her eyes as a black-haired man in a white dress shirt and black pants stepped through the door of a business across the street. Was that Odi leaving his law office? She watched the man lock his door and walk down the sidewalk with a stride almost identical to all the other Robinson men. Shoulders back, striding purposefully to his destination. Even Ori, as laid back as he tried to be, had the same walk.

"Okay." Oscar stepped into the office from a door off to the side, not the door Lucy had entered from the little lobby out front. He sat down in his brown leather chair and pulled it up to the desk. "What do you have to say that can make up for twenty-three years of not being here?"

He was not going to make this easy. Then again, had she made it easy for him when she drove out of his life all those years ago? Did he even remember that day? "Thank you for meeting with me." She pushed her mouth into a timid smile. Oscar propped his elbows on his desk and tapped his fingers together, waiting for her to continue. He should have been the lawyer. "I know you're angry with me, and you have every right to be."

"I'm not angry with you." Oscar's fingers came together. The tapping stopped. "I don't trust you. I'm keeping my distance. I didn't make this decision from an emotional place. I weighed the past, what I know to be true, with what you are claiming is true now. I decided to trust what I already know."

Definitely a lawyer. Lucy cleared her throat and sat back in her chair, crossing her legs. "Almost two years ago, I was diagnosed with breast cancer. I had a mastectomy, chemo, and radiation." She reached up and absently rubbed her collarbone under her blue cotton blouse. "My world changed."

"I get it." Oscar sat back in the chair and laced his fingers together in front of him. "You thought you were going to die, so you decided to come home and make peace with your family. That's all well and good for you, but what about us?"

"No, Oscar." Lucy shook her head, her eyebrows drawing together. "You don't get it. Not at all. While I was in the hospital, the day before the surgery, their chaplain came to see me. He gave me some scripture to read. He kept coming back while I was recovering and met with me while I was doing the chemo and radiation." She reached down and tugged the corner of her skirt. "I started to see who I was—who I really was." She looked down at her hands, searching for words to make her son understand. "I used to be dead, Oscar, just like Lazarus in his tomb. I stunk." She reached up and rubbed under her eye with her ring finger, trying to keep the tears at bay. "I was dead and full of sin and deserved hell... and I didn't even realize it until that chaplain started showing me who I was."

She swallowed again, her throat getting thick with emotion. "I was living only for me, which wasn't life at all. I'm not that way anymore."

"What about what I saw yesterday?" Oscar opened his desk drawer and pulled out a box of tissue. "Here, I usually only have to pull these out during tax season." He didn't smile, but the hard as stone expression was slipping away. "Why were you kissing Cal Warren at the bank while you are engaged to Gordon Blue? Don't tell me God's alright with that, because we both know He's not."

"No, He's not... and neither am I." Lucy pulled a tissue from the box and mopped the tears from her eyes. "Cal took advantage of my surprise. Believe me. I did not invite his embrace at all."

"How do I..." Oscar paused, his eyes searching Lucy's face. The doubt she saw made her heart ache. "How do I know I can trust you?"

"I don't guess you do, really." Lucy pulled in a long breath. "If you will give me even a small chance, I promise I will show you I'm not the person I was. I'm not perfect. Heaven knows I still make a mess of most things, but I'm trying. I'm honestly trying to be the person the Lord wants me to be."

Oscar brought his hand to his face, running his fingers back and forth along his jaw. "I used to cry myself to sleep waiting for you to come home. Daddy would get Aunt Sadie to come rock me while he tended to the rest of the bunch."

"I'm so, so sorry."

"She says I need to give you a chance."

"Sadie said that?" Lucy's eyes stretched wide.

"She said that if I don't forgive you, I'll hurt myself most of all." His lips turned up at the corners. "She said wounds can only fester so long."

"What are you going to do?" Lucy whispered. He looked

so torn, so vulnerable. *Lord, please let him see that I love him and want what's best for him.*

"I guess I'm going to try... to try to be your son." He looked at Lucy, sadness filling his smile. "Please, please don't make me regret it."

"I won't." Lucy stood and stepped around the corner of the desk. Oscar stood up and looked at her. She stopped. "Can I give you a hug? Please?"

"Um." Oscar turned and looked out the picture window to the street, empty and quiet. "I'm not good at that sort of thing."

Lucy reached up and touched his chin, turning his face back to her. "Just stand there. I'll do the rest."

"Thank you for giving up the stage again tonight." Gordon followed Lucy into her hotel room and closed the door behind him. "I guess that's the wrong choice of words. You were still up there, weren't you?"

"How about giving up the spotlight?" Lucy dropped her purse on the bar and stepped to the cabinet. She pulled out a couple of coffee mugs. "Wasn't Ori great?"

"He certainly was. I heard through the grapevine that he may be leaving for Nashville soon."

"Does that grapevine happen to wear a black Stetson?" Lucy poured coffee into the mugs and fixed them the way they drank them, hers black tonight, his with two teaspoons of real sugar. She loved to put cream in her coffee, but not tonight.

Tonight she needed it black and strong. "That man can't keep a secret to save his life."

"Don't be mad at Cal." Gordon took the coffee mug from Lucy's hand as she stepped back to the couch. "He's excited for your son. Almost like Ori was his own flesh and blood."

Lucy's jaw tightened. "What do you mean? He's not—insinuating anything—is he? If he is, I will skin his cowboy behind. He knows that is a bald-faced lie."

"No, no, no." Gordon set his mug down on the coffee table and took Lucy's from her clenched hands. "Not at all. I only meant that he seems to genuinely want to help Ori." He set Lucy's mug beside his and took her hands in his. "Are you okay? Something is bothering you. I can tell."

"Gordon." Lucy squeezed his hands. "I can't marry you." She looked at his face, waiting for his reaction, but he continued to stare at her, his eyes full of the concern she saw when he took her hands. "I love you, but not like I should. You're my friend, but that's all." She waited. "Gordon. Say something."

"I saw this coming." Gordon dropped her hands and sat on the edge of the couch. "I felt it when you first came to Red Creek, but that Sunday, the Sunday he sang in the choir, I knew he had you."

"No, Gordon." Lucy sat down beside Gordon and took his hand again. "He doesn't *have* me. Nobody has me. All Orville did was make me see that it's wrong to marry you out of obligation." She leaned to the side and looked into his down-turned face. "You deserve to be loved. You deserve a woman who will give you her whole heart, who knows you hung the moon, and is willing to do whatever it takes to win your love." She waited. Gordon lifted his face, his eyes tender and sad. "I wanted that person to be me. I tried to be that person. I'm just... not."

"What are you going to do?"

"What do you mean?" Lucy released his hands and picked up her coffee mug. The worst was over. Gordon would be fine.

"Are you going back to Nashville with Cal? Staying here with Orville?"

"Gordon." Lucy swallowed the steaming hot coffee and returned the mug to the table. "Listen to what I'm telling you. Neither Cal nor Orville had anything to do with this. I'm staying here in Red Creek." A knowing look passed across Gordon's face, and she frowned, irritation creeping into her voice. "I'm staying here because this is my town, where my kids are. I'm moving out of this hotel and finding a place. My own place, Gordon. Wipe that look off your face. Orville Robinson has absolutely nothing to do with this decision." *That's not true. You know it, Gordon knows it. Didn't you say you loved him?*

Lucy closed her eyes and pulled in a deep breath, clearing her inner voice from her head. She rolled her head around on her shoulders before opening her eyes. Gordon watched, the same 'I know' look plastered across his face. "I'm tired, Gordon. It's been a long, complicated, and emotional day."

Gordon stood. "You can stay here. You don't have to move."

"I have to." Lucy stood. "I need to stand on my own two feet and not be propped up by you or anyone else." She twisted the engagement ring from her finger and reached for his hand.

"Keep it, Lucy. I bought it for you and you alone."

"You'll find someone else, Gordon." Lucy pushed the ring into his hand. "Give yourself a chance."

She watched Gordon walk out of her room, then flopped onto the couch. Tears filled her eyes as she took another drink of coffee. Why did she feel like she'd been through a war zone? Cal admitted he was the mystery man supporting her all this time. Ori was leaving with Cal tomorrow, heading to Nashville just as she was finally finding her place in Red Creek. Oscar had let her hug him, even if it had been like hugging an oak tree. The break-up with Gordon was done. *Lord, thank you for... sustaining me through all of this. You are my constant, my rock and my truth. I don't know who or what will be in my life tomorrow, but I know You will be. Thank you, Lord.*

Her phone vibrated through her purse over on the bar. She pushed up from the couch, fatigue suddenly weighing her down like a wet blanket. She pulled out the phone and read the text.

> This is Sadie. We need to talk.

The words blurred in front of her as more tears started to flow. Why did making peace, setting things straight, coming to terms with her past—why did it all have to be so hard? She sniffed her nose and wiped her hand across her eyes.

> Tonight?

Little dots started dancing on the screen. Sadie must have been waiting for her response.

> No. How about tomorrow evening? I haven't been to your show yet, but I heard you are doing a great job. We can talk after I hear you sing.

Lucy swallowed down more tears. That didn't sound like a sister-in-law or a fill-in mother who was ready to wring her neck.

> Sounds perfect. See you tomorrow night.

A thumbs up appeared on the screen. Lucy dropped the phone back in her purse and stumbled into her bedroom, not caring that she hadn't turned off the lights or poured out Gordon's coffee. Rest. She needed rest, physical, mental, emotional, and spiritual rest.

Chapter Eighteen

Orville sat down to a breakfast of a left-over biscuit, an egg he scrambled all by himself, and a cup of coffee. His few hours on the creek bank praying and thinking hadn't helped his sleep much at all. The front door opened as he took the last bite of his egg.

"Dad." Owen stepped into the dining room and looked down at his father. "Did you know Ori's going to Nashville with Cal Warren? Did you know he could sing?"

"I found out probably about the same time you did." Orville wiped a biscuit crumb from his scruffy chin. He hadn't bothered with shaving this morning.

"Is it true what Momma says?"

"Your momma says a lot of things. What are you talking about?"

"Momma says Ori is just like you." Owen pulled out a dining room chair, the wooden legs scraping across the old pine floor. "She says Ori sounds as much like you as Oscar looks like you. I heard you singing in church the other day, but Dad, Ori can sing." He waited for Orville to answer. "Dad, is it true?"

127

"Could be." Orville watched his son eyeing his empty plate. "You have breakfast yet? There's another left-over biscuit in the kitchen."

"I'll grab something at the hotel." Owen stood back up. "Won't it be something if Ori becomes famous? Even more than Momma?"

"That would be something." Orville lifted his coffee cup. "Not sure what, but something."

"I've got to run, Dad. Tell Oliver I have a girl I want him to meet." He stopped in the doorway and looked back at Orville. "Scratch that. I'd better tell him myself."

Orville stood and picked up his plate. He'd close the store today. Nobody would suffer if they didn't get to go through a few old WWII metals, or pick through some used tea sets, or decide if a writing desk from the fifties was worth taking home.

He put the plate and cup in the sink and walked into the living room. The mandolin sat in its usual spot on top of the piano. Could Olivia really play it? He picked up the dusty instrument and walked to the front porch. Sadie's truck drove up as he sat down in the old rocking chair. Good. Maybe she'd clean the kitchen. He strummed a few strings on the little instrument and frowned.

"Do you remember how that thing works?" Sadie walked up the creaky front steps and looked down at Orville. "Have you eaten?" She peered at his down-turned head. "I can fry you some bacon and eggs."

"I've eaten."

"Good. I'll go straighten everything up. Heaven knows it'll need it if you did the cooking." She stepped to the front door, opened the squeaky screen, then looked back. "Have you fixed that light switch in the kitchen? It gets hot sometimes when I turn on the lights."

"Not yet." Orville twisted one of the knobs on the mandolin another time, then ran his fingers across the strings.

Sadie raised her eyebrows. "That sounds nice. It's about time you started living again."

"Yeah." Orville didn't look up. If he encouraged her, she'd stand there all day yapping.

"You going to work or gonna sit there and mope all day?" Sadie's hand went to her hip. "After the tourists saw Ori singing at the Blue, a few may want to drop by and see where he works. You might actually turn a profit today... if you go open the place up."

Orville grunted. He plucked on a mandolin string and twisted the knob to tighten it more, not looking her way.

"Okay." Sadie huffed. "Why don't you stay here and fix that light? I'll go run the store when I'm done with the kitchen."

Sadie stepped into the house, the screen door slamming behind her. She'd been picking up his slack for years. She deserved better.

An hour later, Sadie was gone, and Orville still sat on the front porch, picking out a tune on the mandolin. He looked up as Ori's truck bumped down the driveway and slammed to a stop inches away from the metal fence.

"Pop." Ori hopped onto the porch, his long legs skipping the steps. "You should have heard us at the Blue. Mom and I have been singing back-up for Cal Warren." His eyes danced, and he grinned down at Orville. "They even let me sing a couple of times and, Pop, everybody really liked it."

"Is that so?"

"Yes, sir. And now Cal Warren has offered to take me to Nashville with him." Ori shoved his truck keys in his jeans pocket. "I've got to get my stuff from here and Owen's place and a few things from Aunt Sadie's house." He paused and looked around the yard before looking down at his father.

"I'm gonna miss this place." He disappeared into the house, then reappeared twenty minutes later.

"Where'd you spend the night?" Orville laid the Mandolin in his lap and leaned back in the old rocker. "You're leaving today? Right now?"

"I stayed with Owen last night and Cal the night before." Ori picked up the duffle bag he'd dropped on the porch. "I'm not sure when we're leaving, but I want to be ready. Keep your phone on you, Pop. I'll let you know how things are going."

"You do that, son." Orville looked at the guitar strapped to Ori's back. "I hear you can really make that thing sing."

"That's funny." Ori smiled down at Orville and winked. "I've heard the same thing about you."

Orville grinned. "Take care, son." How much had he lost by pushing away the music because it hurt too much? Reminded him too much of her?

"I love you, Pop." Ori squeezed Orville's shoulder. "Don't let Oscar be rough on Momma. She really is sorry for leaving us. Oscar needs to let all that go."

"Your momma can hold her own with anybody, including your brother."

"Maybe so, but still." Ori stepped off the porch. "Keep an eye on her. She's... well, she needs us, Pop."

"I will." Orville watched his wayward son drive away. *Lord, lead him to someone who can lead him to You. You know I've tried, but he won't take the simple path. Guess he's more like me than I care to admit.*

Later that afternoon, Orville watched Oscar's truck coming down the driveway. He didn't need to waste his money on a newspaper, and he sure didn't need to have one of those social media apps on his phone. A phone was a phone. You talked to people on it. It wasn't a TV or telegram service. He learned to text, not that he'd wanted to. Half the time, that was the only way to get his kids to answer their phones. They were great at ignoring him, but when they wanted him to know something, there was no place he could hide where they wouldn't find him.

Orville's stomach growled. He looked down at the silver watch on his arm. Where had the day gone?

Oscar got out of his truck and walked to the porch. "Why are you sitting here in the heat?" He looked down at his father. "Let's go inside. You got any tea?"

"Sadie was here earlier." Orville pushed up from the old rocker, the paint worn away from the arms from years of use. "She probably made a pitcher." He followed Oscar through the door.

"You been out there all day?" Oscar disappeared into the kitchen.

"Yeah," Orville called to Oscar's back. He propped the mandolin in the corner next to the front door then sat down in the recliner. Sitting one place was as good as sitting in another.

"Momma came by to see me." Oscar reappeared through the kitchen doorway and handed Orville a glass of iced tea. He sat on the couch and looked around the room.

Orville sipped his tea and watched his son.

"So." Oscar set down his glass on the coffee table. "What do you think?"

"Bout what?"

"About... all this. Momma being back, trying to be a part of the family again."

"Well." Orville took a long drink from his glass. "She is a part of the family. She's your momma."

"But you know what I mean." Oscar pushed his fingers through the top of his curly black hair. "Can a person really change? What if she up and leaves again? What then?"

"Son." Orville adjusted his hips in the recliner. "The Lord changes people every day. That's what He does. You don't remember the old me before God got ahold of me. If He hadn't changed me a long time ago, before your momma left, you probably would have been raised by your Aunt Sadie. It just, well, it just took your mother a little longer."

"So, you think she's telling the truth? That she's here to stay?"

"I think she's telling the truth about being sorry for leaving us. I think she's telling the truth about giving her life to Christ. Now, whether she stays or not, that's her business."

"What do you mean?"

"Me and you, we haven't really made it easy on her. I don't think Sadie has either. So before you go guessing about whether she's going to stick around, ask yourself if you've given her any reason to stay."

"But." Oscar rubbed his hands together, his eyes looking around the room. He finally looked at his waiting father. "Dad, she did us wrong. For years."

"I know, son. But she's asking for forgiveness, and you're not a kid anymore. You—me— we're grown men, and more than that, we're Christians. We have to forgive her." He stood and wiped the water droplets from his glass. "It's time."

"Where are you going?" Oscar watched his father walk toward the kitchen.

"I'm tired. I think I'm going to go lay down for a while."

"You alright?" Oscar stood. "I don't ever remember you taking a nap, even when you came out of the hospital that time with your heart."

"I'm fine. Go tell your brother goodbye before he leaves for Nashville." He turned and looked at Oscar. "And be nice to your momma. She's trying to do right."

Lucy stepped up on the little stage at the back of the hotel restaurant and looked over at Ori. She was seeing a whole new side of her son, and her worries about him leaving with Cal Warren were fading.

"I've hidden my music from my family for too long." Ori looked at Cal standing in front of the stage area, his hands on his hips. "I want to at least play with Momma one time before we leave. I just wish Pop would come see us."

"You played with your mother for the past two nights." Cal plopped down in a chair at the edge of the stage, watching Ori and Lucy open their guitar cases. "We need to get on the road."

"No. We were playing for you, Cal. This is different." Ori lifted his guitar from its case and raised the strap over his head. "Besides, if you need to leave, go ahead and leave. Momma can get me in touch with the people in Nashville, or I can do like she did and find my own way."

Lucy turned her back on Cal, hiding her grin as she lifted out her guitar. Yeah, Ori was going to do just fine. Owen came in and did a mic check with Ori and her, then opened the doors to the restaurant. The place was going to be packed tonight, but she told Owen to make sure and reserve a table for Sadie.

Her eyes scanned the people filing in to take their seats around the tables covered with white linen cloths. No Gordon, and no Orville. Of course, Orville probably thought Ori had already left for Nashville.

Lucy's face broke into a huge smile. Owen led the rest of

her family, including Oscar, to the front. She stepped down from the stage and started hugging her children.

"Owen texted us about an hour ago and said Ori is singing with you." Olivia hugged Lucy and then Ori. "We certainly couldn't miss that. Quinn is running our restaurant tonight. It will be fun to compare this menu to mine anyway."

"My heart is so full." Lucy's eyes glistened as she embraced her other kids. "Is your father coming?"

"I texted him." Owen shrugged his shoulders. "But Dad is bad about ignoring his phone."

Oh well. She couldn't have everything, but this night was going to be pretty close to perfect. Lucy stepped back up to the stage. She took the mic and looked at the packed room. "Tonight is very special for me. I'm going to be singing for the first time with my son, and future mega-star, Orion Robinson." The room applauded, and she looked over at Ori. He laughed as a few of the locals whistled. She waited for the room to settle down, then sat down on the stool. Ori stood beside her as they started to sing, voices blending perfectly.

As the song ended, several people around the room started to stand. A man near the door waved his hand. "Miss Lucy, I'm a volunteer firefighter and," he nodded to several of the other people rising, "we just got a call-out. It looks like the Robinson house is on fire."

The table up front with the Robinson clan stood, everyone pushing away their chairs and heading toward the exit. Lucy looked around, her mind whirling as people started to talk and move. Ori flew from the stage and was out the side door before she could speak. Was Orville home? Color drained from her face.

"Momma?"

Lucy pulled in a deep breath and looked at her son. "Oscar. Is your father home? He's probably still at the store, right?" She felt her knees buckling under her and Oscar's arms encircled her, stopping her from melting to the floor. "I'm sure he's fine." Her voice caught in her throat as she leaned on Oscar. "Isn't he?"

"I left him a couple of hours ago at the house. He was going to take a nap."

Lucy felt bile rising in her throat. "No. Oh please, no."

"Come on." Oscar urged Lucy to follow Ori's path out the side door. "He's fine, I'm certain, but let's get out there and make sure."

Lucy's mind whirled as they hurried across the parking lot, Oscar dragging her along like she was a doll. Orville... in their house... and the house on fire. She felt Oscar open his truck door and deposit her in the passenger's seat. *Dear God, please, please protect my man.*

Chapter Nineteen

Orville waved his hand through the air, his eyes closed. Who was burning supper? He pushed his sleepy lids up, the grey smoke hurting his eyes. What in the world? He sat up on the side of the bed, clearing his head as he looked around the room in the evening twilight.

Why was he in bed with his clothes on? Why was smoke floating in under the bedroom door? He pushed his hands against his eyes, clearing his vision and his thoughts. He sniffed the smoky air as the day came back to him in a whirl. Yeah, he'd spent the entire day in a pity party, floundering like a baby in his own dejected pit of depression. Enough of that. If one of his kids had tried something like that, he would have taken them to the garden to hoe out their sorrows in the pea patch.

The smoke? What was going on? The heat. A crashing sounded came from the other room, and he jumped to his feet. The hot light switch! Sadie had been after him for a year to get the wiring checked in the old house, but he'd kept putting it off. He hurried to the bedroom door, pulling the collar of his shirt over his nose. He winced as his fingers jerked open the heated doorknob. Tears poured from his burning eyes. Grey and black smoke billowed from the kitchen, eating up the century old hardwood walls and floors like they were cotton candy. He had to get out before it spread to the rest of the house—but....

He pushed his shirt closer over his face and bent forward, holding his breath. He rushed through the hall to the living room doorway. The wall across from where he stood adjoining the kitchen and dining room was yellow and red, flames licking away at his family home. He stepped through the living room doorway and reached above the old black upright piano he had watched his mother play years ago when he was just a boy, back when this was her domain. The gold frame around Lucy's picture was hot to the touch, but he ignored his burning fingers, taking it with him. He started back out the door, but looked down, coughing as the smoke and heat took a toll on his breathing. He reached over and grabbed his guitar propped next to the piano. The twelve strings each seared a new groove into the palm of his hand. He cried out, but didn't let go. The mandolin. Where was it? His eyes darted around through the smoke, the flames moving from the curtains to his old recliner. A crashing behind him sent a wave of heat and sparks in his direction and he hurried from the room.

The smoke in the bedroom looked like a thick smog. He ran in and kicked the door shut behind him. The flames and heat burned closer, taking away everything he held dear. *No, not really. Thank you, Lord, that I am home alone.*

He ran over to the window and set down the guitar and the picture. The blisters already forming on his fingertips sent waves of pain through his hands as he pulled on the window, but it would not open. Nobody had probably opened that window in ten years, since he finally got air conditioning put in on a whim during a particularly warm summer.

More crashing filled his ears, and he coughed, his lungs having difficulty breathing the smoke instead of air. His eyes scanned the sparse room, but there was nothing to break the panes. He leaned forward, coughing, taking him over for a few seconds, then he reached down and grabbed the guitar. It had been his father's, but if he didn't do this, the thing would burn up, anyway. He jerked the afghan off the foot of the bed beside him a wrapped it around the body of the guitar, then rammed it through the window with everything he had in him.

Glass shattered, and he flailed the instrument from side to side, making a hole big enough to climb through. He tossed the guitar as far as he could out into the backyard, then did the same with the picture. The box! How could he forget the box? He dropped to his knees and pulled in a breath of scalding air. His arm shot under the bed and pulled out the old metal box, the flesh on his hands searing in protest. He felt above him and pulled an ancient feather pillow from the bed. Molding the pillow around the box, he pushed it in front of him as he crawled back to the window.

The wall behind him was now flaming. The time had come, get out or go down with the house. He scooped up the box wrapped in the pillow as best he could with the sides of his burned hands and tossed it through the broken panes. Shards of glass pushed into his forearms as he hoisted himself through the hole and tumbled into the grassy bed of daylilies below. Another piece of his mother's life he had taken for granted. Would they bloom next year around the burned down homestead?

Orville rolled away from the edge of the house. He looked around, crawling to the box and the picture a little further out from the burning building. The lid to the box was still closed, thank the Lord. Everything inside it should be okay. He set the picture, bubbling up from the heat, on top of the old box and stood up, pulling his now few possessions to him as he hurried away from his blazing home.

The guitar. He trotted to the edge of the yard toward the

path leading to Red Creek and set down his belongings near the hundred year old oak tree. A siren sounded from not too far away, but it didn't matter. The house was gone. The fire truck might as well turn around and head back to town. His eyes, burning from the heat and smoke, scanned his yard, his vision blurry with tears. The guitar lay a few yards away from the house; the neck broken. He ran over and picked it up, holding it like an injured child. He could fix it. When he did, it wouldn't sit in the corner, forgotten. He would play it. Play it and be thankful.

A spasm of coughing hit Orville, and he leaned forward, pulling in clean air as he staggered back to the oak tree. The headlights of a parade of vehicles flittered through the trees, flying up the long winding driveway toward the house. Orville collapsed onto the ground. The sound of the burning roof crashing down filled his ears, and he lifted his head toward the firelight, the sparks shooting out in all directions. The fire-fighters would make sure the sparks didn't spread the fire to the track of trees separating his place and Sadie's. The coughing started again, and he leaned back, too weak to fight it, blackness pushing him down.

Lucy jerked on the door handle as Oscar's truck flew into the yard. His arm shot out and grabbed her, stopping her from jumping from the moving vehicle. "Momma, wait until I stop or you're gonna break your neck."

Lucy looked out the windshield at the flames, eating away at the charred bones of what had once been the Robinson home. "I don't see him." She leaned forward, her eyes searching through the billows of grey smoke in the evening light. Black pieces of ash floated like death fairies through the air. "Do you see him? I can't see him!"

"No." Oscar opened his truck door. "I don't, but he's not in the house. He's out there somewhere. He got out. I'm sure of it. "

Lucy looked over at her son, his eyes narrow as he searched the front yard between the flaming house and the metal fence in front of them.

Oscar's head turned, looking from the house, almost completely gone, to the tall grass where the firefighters were starting to beat out patches of flames to prevent it from spreading to the nearby woods. "He has to be out there somewhere laying in the grass, and we can't see him."

"But he wouldn't be laying in the grass. Not Orville Robinson." Her eyes stretched wide, and she climbed out of the truck. If he was laying anywhere while his house was burning, that could only mean that he was hurt too bad to get up.

She started toward the fenced-in yard, but a hand reached out and grabbed her arm. "He's not up there, Momma." Ori pulled Lucy back as more firemen began stretching out their hoses and running toward the flames. "I've already checked."

Lucy turned, burying her face in Ori's soot stained shirt. "Where is he, Ori?" Tears poured down her face. Not like this. It couldn't end like this. Orville needed to know, know that it was him. He was the one she still loved, had always loved, would always love.

"Come on." Ori led Lucy back away from the stream of people moving closer to help with the fire. "He's probably out back, or walking over to Aunt Sadie's. Let's get you over there and settled so I can help find him."

"He's back here!" Oscar's voice called through the now noisy yard from somewhere around the back of the house.

"Stay here, Momma." Ori pulled his arms back from Lucy and disappeared down the path around the edge of the yard toward the back of the house. It was the path that led to Red Creek, their path.

"Are you crazy?" Lucy mumbled, hurrying after her son. She bumped into a few men leaving their vehicles and rushing toward the front where the firefighters were working. She didn't slow down, didn't acknowledge them.

At the edge of the backyard, all of her children huddled together, all looking down. Lucy sucked in a gulp of hot, sooty air, pushing down a sob as she ran to where they gathered. She nudged her shoulder in between Oliver and Owen. Orville sat at their feet, his knees pulled toward his chest, hands propped on his knees with the palms facing upward. Olivia squatted beside him, looking at his hands while she talked to someone on her cell phone. Lucy let out a long breath. He was alive. *Thank you, Lord.*

"Daddy, the ambulance is on its way." Olivia pulled her phone from her ear. "They said to lie back down. Don't move."

"I don't need an ambulance." Orville coughed, then looked up at the rest of his kids and finally Lucy. "And it's easier to catch my breath sitting up. None of y'all happen to have a bottle of water in your vehicle, do you?"

"I'll get you some, Dad." Oliver turned and ran back to the front.

Lucy kneeled down in front of Orville. "Back up kids. Give your daddy a little breathing room." She looked at his upturned hands, red, swollen and blistered, the right much worse than the left, but both looked painful. "Your hands are burned."

"Yeah. They'll be alright."

"Are you burned anywhere else?" Lucy eased forward. "Move Olivia. Let me sit next to your father." Olivia stood and stepped back. Lucy scooted to Orville's side. She reached over and pulled a piece of black ash from his head. "This stuff is almost as dark as your hair."

"As dark as it used to be." Orville smiled at Lucy. "It's mostly grey now."

"Is it?" Lucy laid her head on Orville's shoulder, tears filling her eyes. "I hadn't noticed."

Oliver returned and stuck out his arm, giving an open bottle of water to Orville. "Here you go, Dad. It's cold. It should feel good on your throat after breathing all that smoke."

Orville lifted both burned hands toward the bottle. "Here." Lucy took the bottle from Oliver. "I'll do it." She raised the bottle to his lips, and he took a sip, followed by a cough. "You're going in that ambulance, Orville Robinson." She held the water up, and he drank again.

He swallowed the water without coughing this time and grinned at Lucy. "Says who?"

"Says me." Lucy looked at Orville's burned hands. "And when you get out of the hospital, you're moving in with me until you're well."

"Says who?"

"Says me." Lucy raised her eyebrows. "I'm still your wife. You're going to need somebody to make your coffee and shave you and..."

"And dress me." Orville's eyes twinkled. "And give me a bath."

"Would you two please hush?" Olivia rolled her eyes. "You're my parents." She turned. "I think I see the ambulance pulling up. I'm going to go show them where you are."

"Orville." Lucy watched Olivia walk away. She paused and looked around at the boys. "You all go help do something somewhere. I need to talk to your father."

"You heard the woman," Ori said, grinning at his brothers. "Let's go do something somewhere."

"Something useful." Lucy glared at her sons, then turned back to her husband. "Orville." Her finger gently touched his chapped lips. "I need to tell you a few things."

"I need to tell you a few things, too."

"Well, let me go first."

"Mr. Robinson?" Two men with a gurney between them stepped up to where the couple sat on the ground.

"This is your patient." Lucy reached her hand up to one of the ambulance workers, and he pulled her to a stand. "His hands are burned, and he's coughing a lot." She looked down at Orville, scowling up at them. "He's sort of ornery and a little pig-headed, so I'm going to ride in the ambulance with him to make sure he does what he's supposed to."

"Yes, ma'am." The ambulance drivers smiled as they lowered the gurney so Orville could get on. "Sir, do you need us to lift you?"

"Son." Orville glared at the men in their white shirts and black pants. "I wouldn't try that if I were you."

Chapter Twenty

The emergency room doctor ordered chest x-rays, and they took a lot of blood. Orville didn't make a scene through it all, wincing from time to time, but never complaining. Finally, Lucy had enough. "Can't you see he's in pain? I don't care what the man says, he's hurting." She glared at the nurse, who smiled at her patiently.

"Mr. Robinson." The nurse stepped on the other side of the little hospital cot. "Do you need something for pain?"

"Well." Orville smiled and looked down at his freshly bandaged hands.

"Orville, quit trying to impress the girl." Lucy turned her glare from the nurse to her husband. "Tell her to give you something. This is not the time to act like a rooster."

"They are throbbing pretty good." Orville smiled at the nurse. "I could use something if you have it."

"I'll be right back."

The nurse hurried from the room, and Lucy shook her head. "You are plumb ridiculous, Orville Robinson." She pushed her lip up. "I could use something if you have it. Geesh."

Orville smiled. "I sure do like it when you get all hot under the collar."

"Well good. You are going to love me when I start doing the dressing changes on your hands." Lucy was fussing, and she knew it, but tonight had worn on her nerves like nothing else ever had. "Don't even pretend you don't need medicine when we change those bandages, old man, because I know you."

"You do, huh?"

"Yes, you know I do."

The glass door opened, and the nurse stepped up to his cot. She put whatever was in her syringe into Orville's IV. He started snoring a minute later.

Lucy stepped out of the hospital triage room, easing the glass door closed behind her. Why hadn't they given him that stuff to start with? He put up a good front, but his hands had to be killing him. The ambulance worker had placed oxygen on his nose and started an IV before they left the burned down house. He'd given him something for pain, and Orville dozed on the short trip to town, but he moaned every time the vehicle hit a bump, which was often. Whatever this nurse just gave him did the trick...and much better.

Lucy walked out of the triage area and pushed the big silver button on the wall. The heavy wooden doors swung open, leading to the waiting area. She ran her hands through her curls as she walked over to where her kids sat. Did she look as rough as she smelled? Sweat, smoke, and soot covered her clothes, but she didn't really care. Orville was going to be fine.

The children all stood as she stepped up. "He's resting. They finally gave him something for pain. The doctor said they need to keep him overnight to monitor his heart and lungs, but they will release him tomorrow."

"Momma." Oscar stepped toward her; his lips pushed into a flat line. "We need to show you something."

Lucy frowned. "Okay." She looked from one face to the other, but nobody said anything. She turned back to Oscar. "You seem to be the voice of the family tonight, Oscar. What is it?"

"Come out to the truck with us."

"The truck?" Lucy sighed. "Can't this wait? I'm dog tired, and I need to get back to Orville before he wakes up. He can't use his hands, especially the right one."

"This will only take a second, Momma." Ori put his hand on his mother's shoulder. "You'll want to see this."

Lucy's brow pulled low as she looked from one child to the next, each staring back. "Okay, lead the way." She followed them out to the parking lot, where all their pickups were lined up. Oscar took a beat-up black metal box about the size of a Coke crate from his front seat and set it on his tailgate.

"This, the guitar, and the picture of you that hung over the piano, were on the ground by Dad." Oscar looked from the box to his mother. The street lamps made the parking lot glow in a dim yellow light. "You ever see it before."

"No." Lucy frowned. "What's in it?"

All the children stepped in close as Oscar lifted the lid. "Apparently it's where Dad keeps his important... stuff."

"I saw it in his closet one time back when I was a teenager, but Daddy wouldn't tell me what was in it. It had a lock on it back then." Olivia ran a finger along the grungy box lid, soot turning her finger black. "I went back later to try to figure out what was in it, but he had moved it."

Oscar lifted out a Bible. The leather cover was cracked in places from decades of use. He laid it on the truck bed and lifted out the next item. "Look at this bank book. I'm supposed to be the accountant for the store, and I've never seen this account before."

Lucy looked at the little ledger filled with Orville's handwritten notes. She pulled her cell phone from her purse and turned on the flashlight app. "There's..." Her eyes stretched wide at the amount of money showing in the account. "Is this right?"

"We don't know." Oscar shrugged. "But he made another entry a few days ago." He reached over his mother's shoulder and flipped a page in the book. That's the day I saw you and the guy—the day I saw you at the bank."

"But there's." She paused and counted the zeros. "There's over a million dollars here... if this is right. How did your father get that kind of money?"

"That's the really interesting part." Ori looked from his mother to Odi. "Show her those papers." He looked back at Lucy. "Odi says they're legit, too."

"What papers?" Lucy watched Odi lift a faded yellow envelope from the box.

"It appears that Dad has written several songs over the years that made it to number one." Odi opened the envelope and flipped through the stack. "'Head Strong Love,' 'Knock Me Down Again,' 'A Bridge Once Burned.' That's just a few of them."

"Wait." Lucy pulled the papers from Odi's hands. "I thought Cal wrote 'Head Strong Love.' He won a Grammy for it."

"No." Ori shook his head. "I called him a while ago after we started going through this stuff. He recorded it, but didn't write it. Cal accepted the award on behalf of the writer who didn't want to be named years ago when the song won the Grammy. He said rumors started circulating that he wrote it. He said he didn't mean to take credit for writing the song. It just happened. The more I find out about this man, the more I wonder about him. He probably started the rumors himself."

Lucy dropped the papers back in the metal box as ideas clicked in her head. Ori was right to wonder about Cal. He could have never given her that money every month for all those years and not have told her. It would have been impossible for him not to crow about it.

"And look here." Ori opened another envelope. "Me and Owen and Oscar have been trying to figure out ways to make the store turn a profit and stay afloat while Pop was sitting on all this." He pulled out a stack of hundred-dollar bills held together with a paper collar. "There's seven stacks of these in here. Pop is slicker than a wet salamander."

Lucy only half listened as the kids continued to talk. She thumbed through the bank book, looking for routine monthly withdrawals, but they weren't there. Still, the money she'd received was always in cash in an envelope. Did he keep enough out for several months, then only take out more as he needed it?

"Are there any letters? Any documents or... I don't know... anything else in there?" She flashed the light down in the box. "Anything explaining this?"

"There are some letters to a guy named Tucker Frost." Odi pulled a stack of envelopes from the bottom of the box. "I was going to go through them tomorrow, but you can go through them first."

"Tucker Frost?" Lucy's forehead wrinkled. Where had she heard that name? She took the letters from Odi. "I'll get these back to you."

"Momma." Oscar closed the lid of the box. "Your divorce papers are in there too, signed and dated. See the date?"

Lucy bit her lower lip, blinking back the tears. The day Cal Warren had come to town. Had Orville been at the bank that day, too? "What are you going to do... with all of this?"

"I'm taking it to my office tomorrow." Odi looked at Lucy. "Oscar's coming over—and anybody else that wants to, and we're going to sort through everything. You can come too." He picked up three old envelopes he had separated from everything else. "Here. We didn't read these."

Lucy looked at the letters. Letters from her to Orville, promising she'd be home soon, then telling him she needed more time, then asking him to come to Nashville because she couldn't come back. She didn't have to open them. She knew exactly what they said. "Thank you." She blinked back a tear and took the letters from Odi's hand. "I'm surprised he still has these."

"Do you want to be with us when we sort through all of this?" Oscar took a handkerchief from Oliver's outstretched hand and passed it to Lucy.

"No, I need to stay with Orville." Lucy looked down at the box. "Once he gets out of the hospital, he's going to wonder where all this is." She looked around at her children. "What do you plan on telling him? He never has been one to appreciate people trying to mind his business."

"Obviously," Olivia said.

"I'll talk to him." Oscar snapped the latch on the box. "Call me when he starts asking questions."

"I've got to get back in the hospital." Lucy hugged Oscar's neck. *Thank you, Lord, for softening my son's heart toward me.* "Are any of you going to come see him tonight?"

"We all are." Ori hugged his mother. "Call us when they get him to a room. We're going to Olivia's restaurant and grab a late bite. I've got to tell Cal to go on without me."

"Oh, son." Lucy reached up and pushed a blond strand from his eyes. "Are you sure? We will get this all figured out if you need to go ahead and go."

"No." Ori leaned forward and touched his head to Lucy's. "There's nothing up there now that won't be up there after we straighten all this out. Believe it or not, I try to be here when I'm needed."

"Well." Owen stepped over and leaned his shoulder against Ori's. "If you're staying in town, I could use a little help."

Ori raised an eyebrow. "As long as it doesn't involve plucking chickens, I'm your man."

"There's a story there, Mom." Owen grinned at Lucy's confused expression. "I'll tell it to you one day. I was thinking that you are going to be busy taking care of Dad for the next couple of weeks."

"At least that long." Lucy nodded. "But I can handle Orville without Ori's help."

"Yeah." Ori shook his head. "I'm not giving Pop a bath. If that's what is going through your head, big brother, you better think again."

"No, I need you to sing at the Blue every night until Momma is through playing nurse for Dad."

"Now that I'll be happy to do."

"Mom." Oliver stepped past his brothers and hugged Lucy. "We'll bring you food in a while, too. Call us when they get Dad to a room." He glanced back at his sister. "Give Olivia your key to the hotel, and she can get you some fresh clothes, too. Unless you want me to stay with Dad while you go get something to eat and take care of yourself."

"No, I'm going back up." Sweet Oliver. He was always thinking of others. She took her key card from her purse and handed it to her daughter. After another round of hugs, she went back into the hospital.

Lucy stepped into the lobby and walked over to a corner of the room where she could be alone. Before she did anything else, she needed to call Cal Warren. He had never given her any money. He'd introduced her to a few people over the years, people with influence who helped in her career. He always made sure she remembered it, reminding her of how he'd helped make her the star she was. No, he hadn't given her the money. She should have realized that before.

The phone rang, and Lucy tapped her foot against the

floor until Cal picked up. "Lucy, where's Ori? We need to hit the road."

"I'm fine, Cal. My family home is burned to the ground, but thanks for asking."

"Awe, Lucy. I hate to hear that. I was fixing to ask how everybody was."

"I'm sure you were. Now, Cal Warren, I want the truth, and I want it now. If you so much as think about lying to me, I'm going to get Oscar and Owen to pin your sorry hide to the wall."

"Of course, Lucy. There's no need to act like that." Cal chuckled and cleared his throat. "You know I always shoot straight, especially with you."

"Then why did you lie to me about giving me the money over the years? You know good and well you never gave me a dime."

"Honey, you weren't going to let Ori go with me until you had all that figured out, and what did it matter? Really?"

"You... you..." Lucy pushed the red button, ending the call. *Lord, give me the heart to forgive that selfish, hateful man.*

Chapter
Twenty-One

Lucy walked over to the coffeepot near the reception desk and poured a cup of the inky black brew. She needed it strong, but this stuff looked like it could stand up and salute. Oh well. She went back to her corner of the lobby and sat down, opening her purse and pulling out the stack of envelopes. She shoved the three in her handwriting back into her purse and stared at the rest. Some of them were a lot older than the others. One had a brown circle on the front like a wet coffee cup had set on it for a while. She thumbed through the dates to the earliest one in the stack and pulled out the paper. The handwritten letter was in blue ink on faded notebook paper.

Orville,

You're right. Lucy has fallen on hard times. She seems to be making ends meet, but I imagine her landlord will evict her soon. If you're sure you want to do this, I shouldn't have any trouble keeping tabs on her. I've started getting lunch about once a week where she's waiting tables, and she hasn't paid a lick of attention to me. I'll help you on one condition. Promise me you aren't taking food off your own table to do this hairbrained scheme.

Tucker

Tucker Frost. Lucy wracked her brain, trying to remember the man. Seems like she had spoken to him once or twice years ago, but she couldn't be sure. She pulled out the next letter.

Orville,

I'm sorry. I didn't mean to make you mad. I know you can take care of your family. I put the money in an envelope and put it in her mailbox like we discussed. I sat in my usual spot at the restaurant where I could listen around. She didn't mention the money to a soul while I was there, and nobody else talked about it when she was away. I think this may work.

By the way, I heard the demo of your song. That new man, Cal Warren, sounds pretty good, not as good as you or me, of course, but the buzz is that he's got a hit on his hands. Nice going, my friend. You really should come out here and try recording your own songs.

Tucker

Lucy read through a few more letters. Orville had wired Tucker the money every month, then he made sure it made its way to Lucy as he promised. Who was this man? Orville obviously trusted him. According to the first couple of letters, Orville started sending the money before he was getting royalties from his music. Why hadn't he told her? She took a drink of the now tepid coffee. If she'd known back then who the money was from, she would have returned it. Especially knowing it was from Orville. He had needed that money for their family. Why hadn't he told her about it when she came to town? Why keep it a secret now?

She picked up one of the later letters, one from when she was in the hospital.

Orville,

It was good seeing you. When are you going to get a decent truck, friend? I'm surprised that the old thing made it all the way here without breaking down. We both know you have the money to buy anything you want.

I'm glad you came to check on Lucy yourself, but I really wish you would have let her know you were here. She would want to see you, I think. She doesn't have a lot of people visiting besides the hospital preacher. Blue dropped in yesterday and stayed for hours. I'm doing like you said and making sure she's getting the best of everything, but now, so is Blue. You really need to step in on this or Blue is going to steal her away. Tell her, my friend.

Tucker

He'd been to the hospital? Tucker had been there too, apparently often. She picked up the last envelope.

Orville,

I tried to warn you, friend. You could be with her right now if you had just let her know. You could have been with her years ago, I think, too. I agree with stopping the money. I imagine Blue wouldn't let her keep it anyway, no matter how hardheaded you seem to think she is.

I'm pitching our latest song to a couple of folks, and we are getting a bite or two. I think they want to change the title from "Hardheaded Love" to "Our Head Strong Love."

Since you have finally gotten an email account, I'm going to start keeping in touch that way. Let me know if you need me to do anything more with Lucy, but it looks like she is determined to get the divorce and marry Blue. I hate it, but Orville, sometimes you're too stubborn for your own good.

Tucker

PS...you know my phone number. I understand that you hate talking on the thing, but give me a call sometime. It won't kill you. I made those changes to the melody like you suggested on "Hardheaded Love," and you are right. The song flows so much better. That's the way it is on the demo. Good call.

The bed bumped beneath him, and Orville opened his eyes. He squinted into the glaring bright lights above as the ceiling tiles flowed by. "Where am I going?" His voice sounded like a frog. He cleared his throat. "Where's Lucy?"

"She left a couple of hours ago, maybe a little more." The young nurse who had bandaged his hands and given him the medicine that knocked him out smiled down at him as they bumped across the threshold into an elevator. "When she comes back, we'll give her your room number."

"Have my kids been by?"

"No, sir." The nurse looked at the man across from her wearing scrubs in the same color as hers. "He's going to third." The man punched the correct button, and she looked back at Orville. "Your things are in the bag at your feet. If you want me to get your phone out to see if they've called, I can do that for you."

"No." Orville blinked his eyes, sleep and pain medication clearing from his brain. "They can find me if they want to." He listened to the woman talk across the bed to the other nurse or orderly, or doctor, or whatever the guy was. According to their conversation, which they didn't bring him into, he'd been the only one brought in from the fire. It had been a slow night in the ER.

Where had Lucy gone? The way she'd hovered over him in the ambulance and earlier, he'd figured she would have been sitting there waiting for him to wake up. Not that it mattered. He could make it just fine on his own. He lifted his hands, bandaged heavily with white gauze and silk tape, his fingers showing on his left, but not his right. Well, Sadie and Olivia and the others might have to lend a hand and help him with a few things, but he'd get by fine.

The nurse rolled him into his room. She moved him to his bed, put the call light at his side, assured him another nurse would be in shortly, and disappeared. He blew out a puff of air and looked around the room, then down at the bed with the side rails pulled up. Exactly how did they expect him to get up and go to the john? He raised his hands and looked at his bandages, then at the buttons and levers on the bed. He fumbled with the side rail, but couldn't make it do what he wanted, and he was not calling that young girl to come back and help him go to the bathroom. Not today.

He eased his hands under the sheet and blanket across his middle and threw them off. The paper-thin hospital gown stopped at his upper thighs. The sudden draft made goosebumps appear on his hairy legs. *Where did she say she put my pants?* The cool air sent a shiver up his middle. *Great. Now I really need to go to the bathroom.*

He lifted the faded blue gown and looked at his exposed hip, then at the call light. Nope. Even if he did manage to push the button, it wasn't happening. He threw the IV tubing out of the way and twisted, swinging his legs over the side rail, careful not to put much pressure on his bandaged hands. He was over six feet, but still his toes barely skimmed the floor as his knees dangled over the rail. "Looks like I'm gonna have to roll out or bail out." He scooted his naked behind across the bedsheet and as close to the rail as he could. "Getting out of a burning house was easier than this."

Lucy opened the hospital room door, and a thud filled her ears. "Orville Robinson. Have you gone and lost your ever-loving mind?" She hurried to the side of the bed and squatted down beside him. "You could have broken your hip."

"Help me up, Lucy. This floor is cold."

A bubble of laughter floated up from her middle. "Just a minute." The laughter spilled out as she threw her purse on the bed. "Why didn't you call the nurse?"

He looked down at his naked legs, then held up his bandaged hands, his eyes narrow, lips pressed together. "Hurry up. I need to get to the bathroom, and I have no desire to show that young girl my naked behind."

"Oh. Really?" She stood, pushing down her laughter, and wedged herself behind him, putting her arms under his armpits. "Okay." She lifted, and Orville grunted. His hands went to the floor to push up, but he cried out in pain and raised them.

"What in the world?" Ori stepped through the hospital door and started laughing, followed by the rest of the kids. "Do I want to know what's going on here?"

"Hush, boy, and get me up before I wet this floor." Laughter exploded from the doorway.

"Either get in here and help us, or go get a nurse." Lucy raised up and put her hands on her hips. "But quit standing there squawking like a bunch of hens."

The sons hurried to their father's side, easily lifting him from the floor to stand. Olivia shut the door behind them, biting her lips, her eyes twinkling with laughter.

"Grab my pole there, Odi." Orville started toward the bathroom door. "Keep up, son. I'm in a hurry here."

Owen reached behind Orville and pulled his gown together. "Nice dress, Dad."

"Hush, boy, and get my pants." Orville disappeared into

the bathroom with the IV pole behind him. Laughter exploded in the room again.

"Did you talk to him about the box?" Oscar stepped over next to Lucy, his tone quiet as the rest of the family continued to laugh and poke fun at the situation they'd walked in on.

"No, I just walked in myself and found him on the floor."

"Maybe you should wait until you get him to your place. He might handle everything better once he's out of here."

"You are probably right."

"My pants!" Orville bellowed from the closed bathroom. "Now!"

Lucy grabbed the bag from the bed and hurried to the bathroom door. "Orville, if you got the bandages wet, I'm going to skin you alive."

"Tell them to step outside so you can help me with my clothes."

Lucy turned and nodded to the kids. They filed out of the room, and she opened the door. Orville stepped out of the bathroom. She followed him to the hospital bed, pulling his pole behind them. She let down the bed rail. "You have to admit, we were probably a pretty funny sight."

"I don't have to admit anything." Orville sat on the bed and waited while Lucy held his pants at his feet. "How would you feel if they'd come in on you with your behind hanging out for all the world to see?"

"Believe it or not, I've been in a hospital gown a few times myself." Lucy waited while Orville stuck his legs into the pants. "Stand up." She watched, and Orville did as he was told. "There are worse things than flashing your cheeks to your kids."

"Yeah." Orville looked down at the top of Lucy's head, her unruly curls standing on end. "I imagine you're right." He watched her fasten his pants and belt buckle. "I should have been there for you, Lucy."

"We can talk about all that later. Let's get you back in bed." Lucy watched Orville lift his legs onto the bed and use his elbows to scoot up. His hands bumped the bed, and he winced. "I'm calling the nurse. You need some more medicine."

"Wait." Orville reached up toward her face, but stopped and dropped his bandaged hand. "I need to talk to you first."

"You're hurting."

"This is more important." He nodded to the bed. "Sit down for just a second, then I'll do whatever you want."

Lucy eased to the edge of the bed, careful to avoid his hands and not pinch the IV. "Okay, but only for a minute."

"I love you, Lucy. I've already told you that. You said you don't love me, but..."

"I never said that."

"Yes, you did. At the church, and I understand. It's okay."

Lucy's lips turned down. What was he talking about? "Orville, I never said..."

"Lucy." Orville raised his boxing glove sized bandaged hand to her lips. "It's okay. I know you are doing all of this." He looked around the hospital room. "Because you and I have kids together and are... friends."

"Orville. I never said I didn't love you."

"You asked me if you should tell a person you didn't love the truth, Lucy. I remember it. Won't ever forget it."

"I wasn't talking about you." Lucy's eyebrows lowered. "I was talking about Gordon. I was wearing his ring and making wedding plans. I knew I didn't love him. That's who I meant... not you."

"Gordon?"

"Yes. Gordon. It took me a while to get it all figured out, but look." She held out her hand. "I gave him the ring back. See. I'm a free woman."

Chapter Twenty-Two

T he next afternoon, Orville looked over his shoulder toward the bedroom where Lucy had disappeared. "I need you to go to the house." Orville turned and looked at Sadie sitting across from him in the hotel room. "There's a black metal box under the oak tree on the edge of the backyard. Get it and take it to your house."

"What box?" Sadie leaned back on the couch and dropped her purse at her feet.

"It was under my bed. It has a lot of important papers and the song contracts and some letters and things in it. Get my Bible out of it and bring it to me."

"Orville." Sadie shifted her hips and turned to face her brother. "It's time to tell them." She paused, listening as the shower turned on through the wall in the bathroom behind them. "The kids worry about you paying the bills, and Lucy has changed. I can see it; you can see it. Owen said she broke off the wedding with Gordon Blue."

"Keep your voice down." Orville frowned at Sadie. "I'm going to tell them everything, but I need you to get that box before somebody else finds it. There are letters there from

Frosty. I don't want to have people reading those and thinking I was spying on Lucy."

"Well, you were spying on Lucy." Sadie pushed her lips into a flat line and sighed. "But your intentions were good, and your heart was in the right place." She stood from the couch. "Okay, I'll go get your box. Tell Lucy we can talk later."

"Thank you, Sadie." Orville started to stand, pushing up from the arm of the couch with his elbow, but Sadie waved him back down. "You know I'd go myself if I was able, and you're the only one, besides Frosty, that knows everything."

"I know." Sadie leaned over and kissed her younger brother on the top of his head. "You would do the same for me."

Orville watched Sadie walk out of the hotel, then leaned back against the couch. They had gotten to Lucy's place a little after noon. Lucy stayed with him last night at the hospital, waiting on him hand and foot then and again today. She hadn't even gone home last night to get cleaned up. The nurse had come in while she was telling him she'd broken it off with Gordon. Before he could stop the girl, she'd put some more of that good sleeping stuff in his IV.

She'd done it again during the night and again around six this morning before she'd changed his bandages, teaching Lucy how to change the dressing as she went. The rest of the morning had been rushed with the preacher coming by, a home health nurse visiting to schedule future visits, several people from town, including Gordon Blue, stopping in to see how he was doing, and, of course, the kids. If he could have thirty minutes alone with Lucy where he wasn't goofy on pain medicine, he would tell her how he felt. So far, that had not happened.

His phone laying beside him started ringing what the kids called the old-school ring, and he looked at the screen. His family and practically everyone in Red Creek knew about his hands and the house fire. He should turn the thing off. He definitely didn't want to answer it. The name *Frosty* appeared on the screen. Orville looked toward the bedroom. The shower was no longer running. He leaned forward and touched the screen with one of his bandaged fingertips, but he couldn't answer it. After a couple more rings, it finally stopped. He raked the phone closer to him with his paw like hands and scooted it under his thigh.

"What are you doing?" Lucy stepped into the room wearing a pair of baggy grey sweatpants, a white tee-shirt, and her hair wrapped in a towel. "Was that your phone ringing?"

"Yeah." Orville smiled. "I think it was somebody probably checking on me from around... somewhere."

Lucy tilted her head to the side. "Around? Somewhere?" She stepped over to the couch. "You want me to see who it was?" She looked on the coffee table and the couch. "Where's your phone?"

"I've got it." Orville smiled up at Lucy. "It's okay."

Lucy stared down and shrugged. "Okay. If you say so." She reached up and pulled the towel from her head, her curls standing up in every direction. "I'm going to run some bath water for you. We have to put your hands in plastic bags, but everything else needs a bath."

"Everything?" Orville raised one eyebrow. "We?"

"Don't worry." Lucy licked her thumb and rubbed it across a smudge of soot still on Orville's forehead. "I'm not going to invade your privacy, Mr. Robinson. I'll run your water and help you get down to your undies, then I'll step out." She smiled at his skeptical look. "Unless you want the home health nurse to bathe you when she comes by this afternoon? I've seen it all before, but she hasn't." She shrugged her shoulders and leaned forward, replacing the towel around her head. "It's up to you."

"I don't appear to have a choice." He looked down at his

bandaged hands. "How long did the doctor say I was going to be like this?"

Lucy turned at the bedroom door. "You go back to the doctor in a week. He said you shouldn't need all this thick gauze by then."

"A week?"

"A week. We're going to get reacquainted over the next seven days, Orville Robinson, whether we want to or not."

"I want to." Orville's eyes narrowed. "This isn't exactly how I wanted it to happen."

Lucy stuck Orville's bandaged hands in a couple of yellow plastic dollar store bags before taping them securely around his wrists. "I can wash your back and hair if you need me to."

"I'll manage."

"I've seen... it all... before." She pulled his faded white tee-shirt over his head and dropped it on the bathroom floor. Her eyes stretched wide. "Your chest and stomach are scratched up."

"I had to climb through the broken window in the bedroom to get out."

Her fingers gently raked across a purple bruise on his chest, and she swallowed, her mouth suddenly dry. "I'm so sorry this happened."

"It could have been worse."

Orville looked at Lucy, and she looked up into his face, so close. "I'm glad it wasn't."

He leaned closer. "Me too."

His lips brushed against hers, and Lucy's insides flushed

with a fire of its own making. Orville reached up with a bandaged hand, and the plastic crinkled against her cheek. She pulled her lips back from his. "You need to get in the tub before the water gets cold."

"We need to talk." He dropped his hand. "When I get out. Okay?"

"Okay." Lucy nodded. She looked at Orville standing in her bathroom in his boxers, his hands wrapped up like plastic bowling balls, his body scraped, bruised, and burned. "I've missed you, Orville."

"You to." He looked down, suddenly aware of his missing pants. "But I'm not getting in that tub until you step out."

Lucy rolled her eyes. "I never knew you to be the shy type." He lifted a hand and nodded for her to leave. She grinned and stepped out of the room, shutting the bathroom door behind her. She listened. He couldn't really hold on to the wall to step into the tub. He might fall. "You okay?"

"I'm fine."

"Is the water okay?"

"It's fine." Water splashed on the other side of the door. "Go away. I can take a bath on my own. I'm not helpless."

"Call if you need me." Lucy stepped back into her bedroom. Orville had flipped his phone over when he got up a while ago and asked her to slip it into his jeans pocket. He hadn't wanted her to see whoever had called earlier, and that was fine. She wouldn't intrude. They were adults. He could have private phone calls.

She smiled as Orville's rich voice floated through the room singing "Victory in Jesus." *Thank you, Lord, for letting him be okay and bringing me back to him.* She stepped over and looked in the mirror. She was a sight. She hadn't taken time to do what it took to tame her curls. Instead, she'd wrapped Orville's hands in plastic and gotten his bath ready. She looked down at the baggy shirt and lifted it off of her lopsided chest. She hadn't taken time to put her prosthesis in either.

She could at least help herself a little while he bathed. She wanted to stay in the bedroom anyway, just in case he needed her. She opened her dresser drawer and took out the prosthetic breast, lifted her shirt, and slipped it into place in her bra.

She looked in the mirror at the woman before her. Would he even want her when... if he saw the real her? She'd seen him without a shirt and in his boxers. He wasn't the Orville in his twenties that had swept her off her feet all those years ago, but he was still a handsome man. Her heart still did a backflip when he got too close.

She dropped her shirt back into place. He said he loved her, and one thing she knew for certain about the man. He didn't say things he didn't mean. But still. She reached her hand up and patted her crazy curls. He could love her, but still not find her attractive, couldn't he?

"Lucy?" The water splashed from the bathroom. "I might need new bandages. I think I sprung a leak when I washed my hair."

"It's okay." Lucy pulled in a breath of air and blew it out slowly. *I am who I am. I can't be what I was, and I shouldn't want to be. It took doing this to my body to get my soul and spirit and heart where it needed to be.* Orville would do what he would do. She couldn't change what had happened. Didn't want to. "Are you ready for me to come help you?"

The bathroom door opened, and Orville stepped into the bedroom in a pair of jogging shorts, a bath towel around his neck, his hands soppy wet. "Fix my hands, and then we'll talk."

She pushed her lips together, but the corners still tilted up. "I've never seen you in shorts before, especially jogging shorts."

"You never will again when this is over." He looked down

at the flimsy nylon material, a far cry from his jeans. "I appreciate Oscar loaning these to me, but I feel almost naked in these things. The only place they touch me is my waist."

"I don't think your legs have ever seen sunlight."

"Never you mind about that." Orville held up his drippy, plastic covered hands. "Help me fix these. I've got something to tell you, and it can't wait."

"Keep your shirt on." She looked over at the bed and picked up the tee-shirt she'd laid out for him. "Well, how about putting your shirt on? We can talk in a few minutes. I'm not going anywhere, and neither are you. Sit down."

She sat beside him on the bed and started removing the plastic from his bandages. "Orville." She looked at the tape she was unwinding from his wrists. "You know I had breast cancer."

"I know, and that's one of the things we need to talk about."

Her hands stopped, and she raised her eyes to his. "It is?"

"Lucy. I knew what you were going through, and I wasn't there."

A softness filled her chest. "I had been away. A long, long time. I had no right to expect you to be there."

"But I should have been there. You were... are my wife. And." He leaned closer and touched his nose to hers. "And I love you."

"Orville."

A ringing sounded from the bathroom, and Orville pulled back his head. "We have to talk, Lucy. I did some—things— that I need to explain to you."

"Don't you want to answer your phone?"

"No. Not until we talk."

Chapter Twenty-Three

"I'll get it." Lucy stood and walked to her door, leaving the home health nurse to finish up with Orville. When they hadn't answered Orville's phone a couple of hours ago, just after he got out of the tub, the nurse had immediately called Lucy's phone. She wanted to schedule his visit for that afternoon. Since Orville had gotten the gauze wet in the tub, the nurse decided to come right then. She showed up about ten minutes later and was not too happy with what she found. Apparently wet bandages increased the risk of infection and were a big deal.

Orville had been frustrated, wanting to talk, but talking could wait. His health came first. Now, two hours later, the nurse was leaving, and someone else was arriving. Lucy opened the door and smiled at her sister-in-law. "Come on in, Sadie. The nurse is getting ready to leave, so this is a good time to talk." She stepped to the side, and Sadie walked past her. "You want a cup of coffee?"

"No." Sadie stopped inside the doorway. "I can't stay long. Has Orville—mentioned anything to you? About anything?"

Oh. So, Sadie's in on Orville's secrets. "No, not a thing."

Lucy watched Sadie's lips turn down. Lucy opened her mouth but shut it again. She needed to keep quiet. Let the two of them work this out. She would talk to Orville about everything, and then he could do what he wanted to with the information.

Lucy's eyes narrowed. Orville was not going to be happy that she and the kids had gone through his box. If he had not been in the hospital room resting, they wouldn't have opened it without him. They were looking out for him. Whether he saw it that way remained to be seen.

Lucy followed Sadie into her living area but didn't sit down. The nurse stood, ready to leave. Lucy turned and walked with her back to the door. Orville and Sadie obviously wanted a minute alone. She would give them that. Besides, she still wasn't sure how to approach the subject of the past twenty-three years. How did she admit to her husband that she was okay with taking money from a stranger for all that time? *You start off by telling him you are not that woman anymore.*

Lucy said goodbye to the nurse, promising to keep the bandages clean and dry, then turned. "Oh, goodness." Lucy stopped, nearly bumping into Sadie. "I didn't see you behind me. You leaving already?"

"I am." Sadie's brow furrowed. "At first I was suspicious about you coming back, but I've decided if you can put up with that pig-headed brother of mine for any amount of time, you have to be a good woman." She rushed past Lucy and the home health nurse, not bothering to say goodbye.

Lucy leaned out the door and watched the nurse walk down to where Sadie was waiting for the elevator. What in the world? The two stepped into the elevator and disappeared.

"Lucy!" Orville's voice bellowed from the couch. "Shut and lock that door and turn off the phones. We need to talk.

Now. I don't care if Red Creek falls down around our ears. We are going to talk."

"Here we go."

Orville watched Lucy turn and walk back to the living area. "Lucy, come here. There's a lot I need to tell you." He waited while Lucy sat down. She didn't say anything as she leaned back on the couch and looked at him, her eyes calm. "I didn't mean to yell."

"I think you need to apologize to your sister. She didn't seem too happy when she left."

"Probably." Orville reached up to rub his jaw. His right hand was pretty much useless, wrapped up like a giant oven mitt. He frowned and raised his left hand. His fingertips stuck out, each wrapped in their own thin layer of gauze. He rubbed his whiskers. He would have to grow a beard. After he let this cat out of the bag with Lucy, he wasn't letting her come near him with a sharp object, especially a razor—especially near his throat. "I'll talk to Sadie when we're done."

"Okay." Lucy slipped off her sneakers and tucked her feet under her thighs. She smiled. "I like you a little scruffy, but I can tell it's bothering you. Do you want me to shave you while we talk?"

"No." Could she read his mind? It seemed like she did back in the day. No, she was smiling. If she knew, she would not be smiling. "Lucy, when you left that day, I should have followed you."

"Orville."

"Please." Orville reached out his hand. *Confounded bandages.* He pulled it back. "Let me say what I need to say."

169

Lucy adjusted her shoulders against the couch and nodded. "I should have packed up the kids and gone with you, not send you off alone. I knew you wanted to do that before we met. You had your heart set on trying to make it as a singer, but I ignored what you wanted. All I thought about was me."

He turned on the couch, scooting closer to where she sat. "When you said you wanted to go, I used the kids, our obligations, the store, all as excuses to do what I wanted. That store wasn't paying the bills. I was always working at the dairy, or the sawmill, or wherever to pay the bills. I could have done that in Nashville... with you by my side."

"Orville, I..."

"No." Orville held up his hand. "Let me get this out. Do you remember Frosty? The guy that played bass for my band back in high school?"

"Yes." Lucy's eyes stretched wide. "Frosty. I do." A strange expression filled her face.

"He moved away right after he graduated high school." Orville's eyes narrowed. Why was she looking like she'd just won the lottery?

"I remember. I had forgotten all about Frosty."

"He and I kept in touch after he was gone." Orville pulled in a deep breath and looked around the room, way too fancy for his taste. "Anyway, at first, I figured you'd be back home by the end of the month." His eyes pulled back to Lucy's face. "I guess I thought you couldn't make it... without me."

Lucy's mouth turned up in a smile, but she remained silent.

"When you didn't, I looked up Frosty. He was living in Tennessee, outside of Nashville. He found out where you were living, and..." Orville's lips pushed together in a thin line. "Well, I started spying on you, Lucy."

"Spying on me?"

"Yes, spying on you. I got Frosty to find out where you

were working and living. He would call me or write to me to let me know how you were doing. Make sure you were okay."

"Orville, you could have come and checked on me yourself."

"Well." Orville swallowed. "I did a few times."

"A few times?" Lucy's eyes stretched wide again. "When? Why didn't you—talk to me?"

"The first time I came, you were sitting at that place where you worked as a waitress, laughing and talking with Cal Warren." Orville spat the name out like it was poison. "I figured you'd moved on, so I turned around and went home."

"Orville." Lucy scooted closer. She reached up and stroked the day's growth of whiskers along his chin. "We've both been so stupid."

"There's more, Lucy." Orville reached up with his left hand, the one that wasn't like a boxing glove. "Frosty told me about the rat hole you were staying in."

"I wouldn't have called it a rat hole."

"That's how Frosty described it. It hurt seeing you with *him*. But I couldn't let you live like that, so I sold a few acres of the home place to Gordon and started sending you money every month... through Frosty." He paused, his eyes searching her face. She didn't look nearly as shocked as he figured she would. "Then later, when I started making a little money, I bought the land back."

"I know."

"I sent you money every..." Orville stopped. "You know?"

"Yes, Orville." Lucy smiled. "I know. The boys found your box and showed me everything in it."

"The boys have the box?" Orville's eyes widened. "Thank the good Lord." His shoulders slumped against the couch. "I thought for sure one of the first responders had found it and threw it in the trash."

"There was a lot of money in that box along with your bank book."

"Yeah, and my Bible and some letters and…" He reached up and touched Lucy's face with his gauzy fingertips. "And our divorce papers. Lucy, are you sure that's what you want? If it is, the papers are signed. I'll quit fighting you if it's what you truly want."

"Before we get to that, I want to ask you a couple of things… and tell you some things."

"Alright." Orville dropped his hand. She didn't look furious or disappointed. "I'm listening."

"First of all, what I did was wrong. I never should have left you and the kids."

"But it was your dream…"

"My turn." Lucy raised a finger and placed it on Orville's lips. A tingle ran down his spine. He reached up to take her hand, but she pulled it down and backed across the couch. "Oh, no. You have to listen to me like I listened to you."

"I wasn't going to do anything." Orville smiled, his eyes twinkling.

"Of course not. Anyway," Lucy tucked a curl behind her ear. She pulled in a deep breath and blew it out through pursed lips. "I didn't know who was sending that money. I knew you probably hated me for leaving."

"I…"

Lucy held up her hand, cutting Orville off. "And I knew you didn't have any money to send. I was desperate. I took the money the first time, promising myself that I'd figure out where it came from and pay it back. But then it came again and again. I became dependent on it for several years." Tears crowded her eyes, and she looked down at her hands. "I felt dirty taking it, like a kept woman."

"Lucy."

"No, Orville. I shouldn't have taken it. I didn't know where it was from or what someone was expecting in return, and I took it anyway." A tear rolled down her cheek. "Every time I took that money, I felt myself slipping away from you, the wife and mother I was supposed to be. When my singing started paying the bills, I pushed the ideas away. I stayed on the road and kept busy, but when I got home, the money would be there, waiting."

"I'm so sorry." Orville looked at the tears on Lucy's cheeks, and his heart squeezed. "I never meant for it to be like that."

"I know." Lucy cleared her throat. "It's sort of ironic. If you hadn't sent the money, I probably would have come home with my tail between my legs years ago." A corner of her mouth turned up in a lost smile. "But God had a plan for us, even while we were both busy making a mess of things. If I'd come home then, I'd still have been as lost and hell bound as I was when I left."

"Lucy."

"It took the cancer... me losing everything I thought I could depend on to let me see who I could really depend on." She swiped the back of her hand across her cheek. "God came to me and scooped me up in His arms when I couldn't even lift my own head off the pillow without vomiting my guts out."

"I should have been there."

"That wasn't God's plan, Orville. You know how hard-headed I am. It took losing everything. Me chunking away my family, and God ripping away my career to bring me to where I saw who I was and who He was. I regret a whole lot, but... I'm also thankful."

"Will you forgive me?" Orville slid closer to Lucy and wrapped his arms around her. "I let my pride and selfishness drive a wedge between us."

"So did I." Lucy laid her head on Orville's shoulder. "Daddy always said we were too much alike to live together."

"He's wrong. We may be alike." Orville's bandaged fingertips ran down the side of Lucy's upturned face. "But I don't ever want to live without you again."

"Orville." Lucy sat up and pushed away where she could see his face. "There's one more thing."

"What's that?"

"I understand why you kept the money thing a secret from me all these years, but why after I came back? You wouldn't give me a divorce, but you didn't tell me about taking care of me, either."

"I was sure you didn't love Gordon Blue. It was as plain as the nose on your face. I wasn't sure why you were marrying him, but I figured it had something to do with him and the cancer and him being there for you." Orville leaned back against the couch. "I didn't want that with us."

"What?" Lucy's hand reached up and tugged on the neck of her shirt. "What do you mean?"

"I didn't want you to come to me out of obligation." Orville looked down at his useless hands and smiled. "It's ironic. I wanted you to come to me because you loved me. Loved the man I was. No other reason. Now, here we are. I'm in your house... Gordon Blue's hotel... because you are taking care of me. I'm here because I have no other place to go and nobody else to lean on."

"That's not true." A mischievous grin crept across Lucy's face. "I'll make Owen take you in, and get Ori to give you your baths. Oscar and Odi can change your bandages, and Olivia and Oliver can feed you and do your laundry."

"Over my dead body."

"Orville," Lucy scooted back over and laid her head on his shoulder. "I thought I lost you in that fire and... my world fell apart. I love you. I don't care about your hands or where we live. I want to be with you wherever you are. Rich or without two pennies to rub together, I don't care."

"I'll go back to Nashville with you, Lucy. If that's what you want." Orville stroked her hair. "Home isn't a house or even a town. It's being with the person you love. I love you."

"I love you too, Orville."

Epilogue

"Shoo that chicken off the concrete, Olivia." Lucy looked around the yard. The past three months were wonderful in most ways, difficult in a few. Moving out of the Blue Hotel and into a travel trailer at the Robinson homestead had been... interesting. Orville only owned the clothes on his back, so the move started him off in a new home and in a new wardrobe. The travel trailer was nothing like his old family home, obviously, but the clothes. They made a trip to the co-op and bought five pairs of wranglers and five button-up work shirts exactly like the ancient ones he lost. Some things were written in stone, and Orville Robinson's sense of propriety with his clothing choices was one of them. Lucy managed to talk him into a pair of black jeans, new cowboy boots, and a white dress shirt for Sundays... and today.

She looked at the slab poured in preparation for the house they were building. It was not exactly where the old house stood. They moved their future home back a bit to catch the shade of the giant oak tree in the corner of the yard. Some of the hard things had been watching her children come to terms with the loss of the home they grew up in. Lucy wanted to build a house big enough to accommodate Oscar and Ori and Oliver, the three who still lived in the old house before the fire, but Orville put his foot down and said no.

"It's time for us, Lucy. All three are grown and have decent jobs. They can build on the property if they want. I'll even give them some land and help them build their houses. I want this house to be ours, yours and mine alone."

How could she say no to that? A home of her own with her family nearby? She couldn't. Ori stayed in Red Creek for a month until he was sure his pop was going to be fine before leaving for Nashville. He'd returned last night, but only for the weekend, only to be gone again. One day he'd be home for good. Lucy understood his need to chase a dream. *Lord, lead him to You. I pray his path to You is a bit easier than mine, but I trust You to bring him home.*

"You ready?" Olivia, wearing a blue sundress, fitted at the top and falling in waves at the empire waistline nudged her mother.

"Ready." Lucy looked at her daughter and smiled. She sure had been wearing a lot of loose tops lately. Was a baby on the way? She turned and faced her husband, walking up from the nearby travel trailer. This little ceremony was not what most women would want for their vow renewal, but Lucy Robinson was not most women. She'd tried the glitz, the glamour, and all that went with it. It was fun for a while, but deep down, none of that mattered.

Here, on their future home site, surrounded by family as her son played his guitar, Lucy knew she was exactly where God intended her to be, and she felt peace.

Orville walked across the concrete slab where his new forever home would be and smiled down at Lucy. He'd made peace with himself and the kids and his wife. He'd kept his songwriting success a secret, not out of spite, but out of love. He loved his life in Red Creek, and he hadn't wanted it to change. God; however, had other plans, better plans.

He'd written the lyrics and music to "Head Strong Love" when Lucy quit calling and answering his calls. Eventually, he showed the song to Frosty, who thought it would be a hit. Hearing Cal Warren, the man who he thought had stolen away his wife, sing the very song he wrote about losing her, had almost driven him insane. He'd put down his guitar and didn't pick it up again for all those years.

After that, from time to time, Frosty would ask him if he had any lyrics. He'd send them to his friend, who would then write the music. They'd made a good living that way through the years, but no song ever did as well as "Head Strong Love." He didn't care now that the world thought Cal Warren wrote it. None of that mattered anymore. He had the headstrong woman back. That's what mattered.

They were already married, had been for decades. Today; however, started a new chapter. "Reverend, let's get this started. Me and this beautiful woman have a honeymoon to get going on."

"Honeymoon?" Lucy looked up at Orville. "You haven't mentioned a honeymoon." She looked from Orville to the kids, who all shook their heads. "Where are we going?"

"I thought we'd take the house on wheels and make a little

road trip. When we get back, our new place should be just about finished."

"I don't know." Lucy's lips poked out. "I'm not sure your old truck will pull the fifth wheel. I really don't want to break down on the side of the road. My truck's not big enough to haul it either."

"I've taken care of that." Orville turned as a shiny, new, black one-ton pickup truck rolled up the driveway with Olivia's husband behind the wheel. "I couldn't trust none of our bunch to keep a secret, but Quinn can be tight-lipped when he needs to be."

"That's yours?" Lucy's head jerked back to her husband.

"Nope." Orville smiled. "It's ours. No more yours and mine. Everything I own is yours too, Lucy Robinson, including my heart. Now, let's get this show on the road. The leaves in the mountains are supposed to look nice this time of year."

Thoughts about the story...

I always look for inspiration for my books, or themes for my books from the Bible. This story developed after studying Acts 9. Can you imagine being Saul after he was blinded by a vision from God? He was helpless, humbled, and completely changed. He was no longer the ruthless murderer he had been, praise the Lord, but a new creation through the power of Jesus.

But here's the kicker, the part that makes me get a knot in my stomach every time I study it. The Lord said he was going to suffer much for Him. That's not what gets me. What truly gets me is that the Lord sent Saul back to the very people he had been murdering in the streets to proclaim the gospel. "Uh, hello. I'm Paul. Formerly Saul... the guy who stoned your grandma last week. Can I tell you what Jesus has done for me?" Ouch. That had to be a mind-blowing idea, not only for Paul, but for the Christians the Lord sent him to witness to.

That is where the idea of Lucy Robinson came from. I tried to think of the most horrible thing a woman could do to her spouse in a Christian woman's eyes, and Lucy's past was born. Then, I somehow had to redeem her to the very ones she had hurt. When I told my daughter that Lucy abandoned her babies and husband to seek fame and fortune, my daughter said that would be impossible to come back from.

That's what I wanted. Because, just like Saul of Tarsus, who became Paul the apostle, Lucy was transformed, not of her own doing, but through the power of the blood of Jesus Christ. So tell me. Did I pull it off? Did you cringe when you found out she walked out on her babies? I sure did. When Orville told Oscar to forgive her because he was a Christian, did you wince a little? I did.

Let me know what you thought. Read Acts chapter nine now and ask yourself what Paul and Ananias went through that day on Straight Street.

Blessings,
KC

A Little About KC

KC sincerely believes that well-written Christian fiction can change lives. When a novel has strong Christian principals woven intricately into a well-written plot, the reader bonds with lifelike characters who struggle with trials, temptations, and struggles that the reader identifies with. The reader identifies with these characters because she's been there. Everyone has fallen. That's why everyone needs a Savior.

Then, when these same characters turn to Christ the Savior to bring them through these dark moments, the reader finds hope. KC believes the story reminds the reader why she must lean on the Lord in her trying situations. Through the book's structure showing Christianity as the positive light for good that KC knows to be true, the reader also sees why she needs to be the hands and feet of Christ to others.

KC strives to show how the Lord uses situations, people, and His Word to bring the lost to Him, and mold, prune and grow His children. She tackles challenging situations, powerful emotions, and spiritual warfare through engaging stories and true-to-life characters.

KC's favorite Bible verses are Philippians 2:5-8. Have this mind among yourselves, which is yours in Christ Jesus, who, though he was in the form of God, did not count equality with God a thing to be grasped, but made himself nothing, taking the form of a servant, being born in the likeness of men. And being found in human form, he humbled himself by becoming obedient to the point of death, even death on a cross.

KC cannot read these words without getting a lump in her throat. She strives daily to use her writing, her platform, her small influence to show others the love Christ has shown her.

If you enjoyed this book, please take a few minutes to leave a review. Authors, myself included, really appreciate this, and it helps draw more readers to books they may enjoy as well. A few words are appreciated...
Thanks! KC

Join KC's newsletter and receive a free ebook of Music Smarts and Humble Hearts

Follow KC on her social media platforms

https://www.goodreads.com/author/show/20570083.
K_C_Hart

https://www.bookbub.com/profile/kc-hart?list=
author_books

https://www.facebook.com/KCWRITESBOOKS

Also By
KC Hart

A Christmas Blaze

Fresh Starts and Small Town Hearts

Business Smarts and Reckless Hearts

Car Smarts and Bashful Hearts

People Smarts and Wounded Hearts

Kid Smarts and Wistful Hearts

Family Smarts and Runaway Hearts

Elsie: Prairie Roses Collection

Moonlight, Murder and Small Town Secrets

Music, Murder and Small Town Romance

Memories. Murder and Small Town Money

Merry Murder and Small Town Santas

Medicine Murder and Small Town Scandal

Marriage, Murder & Small Town Schemes

Mistaken Murder & Small Town Status

Mistletoe, Murder & Small Town Scoundrels

Join KC's newsletter and receive a free ebook of Music Smarts and Humble Hearts

If you enjoy my books, please consider leaving a review where you purchased them. Reviews help an author in so many ways.

Blessings,

KC Hart

Made in United States
Troutdale, OR
05/17/2024

19947627R00108